HALF
MOON
STREET

HALF MOON STREET

TWO SHORT NOVELS

PAUL THEROUX

HOUGHTON MIFFLIN COMPANY BOSTON 1984

Library of Congress Cataloging in Publication Data

Theroux, Paul.
  Half Moon Street.

    Contents: Doctor DeMarr—Doctor Slaughter.
    I. Theroux, Paul. Doctor Slaughter. 1984. II. Title.
PS3570.H4A6   1984   813'.54   84-10495
ISBN 0-395-36511-2

Printed in the United States of America

Q 10 9 8 7 6 5 4 3 2 1

DOCTOR SLAUGHTER

1

At first Lauren had liked being new to London and not knowing a soul. Being a stranger was a thrill, like being in disguise — full of those possibilities. And she believed that strangers were among the few people in the world who could be trusted with the truth. She loved telling them her secrets, and discovering theirs. But the city, so far, had disappointed her: London wasn't London. She had not seen anything here that she had expected, and after a month she had seen too much that she had never expected.

This morning she was standing in her freezing room, wearing her mink-lined coat, thinking about the General's dinner party — the incredible thing the guest had said.

"There are five thousand people in the world." And he had smiled at those on the left of the table, then — taking his time — those on the right. Finally, his eyes came to rest on the woman who had been saying "absolutely" all evening. She did not say "absolutely" now.

The people at the table offered one of those silences that are intended to let a man finish. It had certainly seemed like an unfinished sentence. But the man just smiled again and lifted his knife and worked it through the fist of meat bleeding on his plate.

She had found out his name during the first course. Taking her fork out of her mousseline she had pointed it at the wall just behind the General.

"That painting looks like a Van Goh," she said.

"Van Goff," the General said.

"Fon Hokh," the man said, and then, "I should know that, as a Van Arkady."

He had done more talking than the host. At these London dinner parties the host often seemed the least important or the quietest person in the room. The host was interesting only because he brought much more interesting people together — so it seemed to Lauren. General Sir George Newhouse, head of the Hemisphere Institute, was famous for his guests and famous for saying very little. He had only opened his mouth once tonight and that was to mispronounce the name of the Dutch painter. But it had hardly been noticed, for Van Arkady was still talking. They were now on the main course.

He said, "That's it. The population of the world. Five thousand."

They had been discussing recent catastrophes — the scale of them in human lives: almost a million dead in the Ethiopian famine, half a million refugees in Lebanon, ten thousand throats cut in a massacre in India, and in the most

4

recent Chinese earthquake upward of two million either dead or homeless.

The Chinese statistic was Lauren's, and when she said it (someone whispered, "I had no idea there was an earthquake there last year!"), Van Arkady stammered for attention and then delivered his pronouncement about there being five thousand people in the world.

It sank in — he meant just that. It was a very London way of speaking — abrupt and cynical and knowing, like a polite way of starting trouble. Lauren had once asked General Newhouse about a certain Arabic scholar and the General shrugged and said, "He doesn't exist." And when you cut someone at a party, she had been told, it was not that you were ignoring the person or that you were turning away — it was that the person was not there: you saw nothing. It was all a London manner she was trying to get used to.

Everyone turned to her when Lauren said, "China's population has officially reached one billion."

"That's official," Van Arkady said. "I am speaking of reality."

"Yes, in reality there are a billion people in China."

"Wrong," he said. "There are two people in China." He was smiling at Lauren. "I know both of them."

"I never touch salt," Lauren said to the man next to her who was offering her a little hopper of salt with a tiny spoon stuck in it. "But if I did, I certainly wouldn't spoon it out of that thing." Then her face became radiant and she smiled at Van Arkady. "Two people in China. I love it."

"I've been to China," Van Arkady said.

"Everyone's been to China," Lauren said, still smiling.

Lady Newhouse said, "Hugo, did it ever occur to you that you might not be one of those five thousand?"

"The thought never entered my head," Van Arkady said.

Lauren at that moment seriously wondered: If he's right, am I one of them? It did not come in words. She saw herself fleetingly in half shadow as a small dim rejected figure without a face. She worried for a few uncertain seconds that Van Arkady might be joking. He had talked the whole time, acting as host — pouring wine and pronouncing. Who was he?

The others had become nervous; the conversation had faltered. She hoped it was not a joke. She could not see a joke in it. It was so extraordinary she wanted it to be true.

"And I have a theory," Van Arkady said — and people relaxed a little, glad that he was managing all the talk; he was ugly and interesting, about her father's age, but dark; and what sort of name was Van Arkady? "This theory is that if you live long enough you meet them all."

"It's a metaphor!" Julian Shuttle said — too loud, he was very angry and speaking to the table at large. He was young, about thirty, and had recently been asked by General Newhouse to join the Hemisphere Institute. When Lauren told the General that she had decided not to study China, as she had planned, but to start from scratch on the Persian Gulf, she was put in Julian's office. Julian was an Arabist. Lauren suspected that the General was trying to frighten her into resuming her studies of the Chinese economy. But Julian was not the sort to intimidate her, and when she said that she didn't know anything about the Gulf he said, "Don't worry about it. That's what fellowships are for." He was kind and intelligent, and although he was Lauren's age he had an endearing way of behaving like her younger brother.

"A metaphor?" Van Arkady said. "No, it is not that at all." His manner was patronizing. He did not insist and it made him seem very sure of himself. "It is a fact. I can name many of them."

"Carry on," Julian said, looking nervous and bold.

Van Arkady said, "The names would mean nothing to you, young man."

Lauren admired the man's roosterish arrogance. When she was impressed her face shone, the excitement whipped up her blood and made her prettier. And the man's arrogance somehow went with his ugliness and made him majestic.

"What about the rest of the people in the world?" Julian asked. His voice cracked a little — he was upset, and he seemed beseeching rather than challenging.

Van Arkady ignored Julian. He turned to the other dinner guests. But he answered Julian's question. He said, "The rest don't really matter. A million dead here, two million there — it is part of a natural cycle. Yes, even massacres. There is murder in nature. Please don't think I'm insensitive. I believe the death of one man can change the course of history, when it is the right man and when we are fully conscious of it. But a million don't matter, because it isn't a number in any actual sense, unless it is applied to money. A million dollars is an easy thing, but a million men is impossible to imagine. My five thousand is reality, but" — and here he smiled at Julian Shuttle — "a million men is a metaphor."

Julian seemed to sulk at this, and at the end of the table Mrs. Timothy Beach whispered, "My cleaning lady said, 'A blue foulard — that's a kind of duck, isn't it?' "

"We don't feel a million," Van Arkady was saying. "You can't honestly say that you miss all those Ethiopians and Chinese. Their deaths don't change anything, and a truthful but callous person might argue that we're all a jolly sight better off without them. We make a pointless virtue out of keeping people alive. It is one of the follies of our century — it is a mere conceit, making us feel powerful. But it is sometimes much kinder to allow people to die in their own way than to keep them alive our way."

Lauren was thrilled at this — not the details of the argument but the calm cruel way the man stated it, and she wanted him to notice her approval.

Over dessert it became a game. How many of the five thousand were British or German or African? Van Arkady considered each question seriously and answered "Forty-five" and "Sixty" and "None."

He said, "And more Arabs than you might think."

"I do Arabs," Lauren said.

"The ones I am speaking of are all here in London."

"In other words, no Bedouin," Lady Newhouse said.

"What is a Bedouin?" Mrs. Beach asked.

Lauren said, "They're people who like to live in tents."

The man on Lauren's left — Giles something, from the Foreign Office — said, "Aren't you going to eat your syllabub?"

"Is that what it's called?" Lauren said, and she laughed out loud. Then she said, "No, I kind of watch my sugar intake."

"And you didn't touch your duckling."

"I don't eat meat," she said.

"Did you know Hitler was a vegetarian?" he said, and he scowled and made his eyebrows devilish. Then he relented. "So was George Bernard Shaw."

Lauren said, "I've never read him."

"You've missed something," the man said.

"No. I'll never read him. I think it's very unlucky to read Shaw's books. My uncle was reading a book by him when he died."

Lady Newhouse stood up and said, "Anyone who would like to —"

"I'm going to miss you," the man said.

"I'm not going anywhere," Lauren said.

"You're being summoned," he said. "Ladies to the loo, while the men pass the port and cigars around."

"What a nerve," Lauren said softly. "And this is a black-tie dinner."

"The General is very old-fashioned."

"To me that always means a complete asshole."

The man began to stifle a laugh, and then he gave in to it and said, "But you don't drink!"

"You notice everything," Lauren said. "Anyway, it's the principle I object to."

"Or do you want a cigar?" He had taken two thick cigars out of a leather wallet and he held one under her chin.

"Where I come from," she said, "we call that a sour dick."

She was taken to a narrow parlor-like room with the five other women and they took turns using the adjoining toilet. One by one, they spent far too long behind the door and returned with different faces — like masks made of pastry flour and food coloring: the first time Lauren heard the word "tarts" she thought of the glazed and frosted faces of these old women.

But one wore no make-up. She was a frog-faced woman who wobbled in her shoes and when she took her turn in the toilet the other women exchanged glances. Lauren suspected it was Van Arkady's wife.

"Five thousand people," one woman said, mocking the man by making his accent seem foreign.

"He is so full of himself," Mrs. Beach said.

Then Lauren was sure that the frog-faced woman was Mrs. Van Arkady.

"Ginnie," Lady Newhouse cautioned.

But Mrs. Beach, who was seated in a chair next to Lauren, was still talking in a low defiant voice.

"He's a fornicator," she said.

Lauren laughed, and when she saw Van Arkady again in the Newhouses' drawing room — they were having coffee — she wanted to go home with him. His ugly wife was a burden to him — she looked unhealthy and bad-tempered. She certainly wasn't one of the five thousand!

"What do you do?" Lauren said to Van Arkady.

The question surprised him, but he looked pleased and said, "I'm just one of these boring bankers."

Lauren said, "I find money incredibly exciting."

"I sometimes think that money has no existence," Van Arkady said. "It is simply something that certain people believe in — and they have given it a kind of temporary reality. It is a bubble — it must be, because in the past it has actually burst. And of course that will happen again."

He was edging sideways as he spoke, moving Lauren toward the fireplace, where logs were flaming — she could feel the heat against her legs.

"And what is your profession?" Van Arkady said.

She said, "I do just about everything."

"Surely not everything," he said, dropping his voice.

"When I feel like it," Lauren said lightly.

Just then, Mrs. Van Arkady — small, sallow, with shins like knifeblades and wearing big blue shoes — stepped over and claimed her husband, who was still smiling and a little breathless from the way Lauren had seemed to dare him.

But men were so slow, and she felt she always had to do all the work and make it easy for them, and then she had to seem surprised when they at last made a move.

She watched the Van Arkadys go to the foyer, and to be persistent — to show herself again — she went downstairs after them and found her own coat, and waited to be asked whether she needed a lift. But the ugly woman had probably said something to her husband, because he looked a little sheepish and only said, "What a wonderful coat," and helped her on with it. She wanted to face him and say that she believed that she was one of the five thousand he had spoken of.

But instead she said, "Thanks" and let her gaze linger on him. He was a cruel and henpecked man — but just like her father, and like many men, who were savage and brilliant in company, but at home they wore aprons and called their wives "Queenie" and got furious trying to be helpful.

Lauren saw herself as he must have seen her — standing in her warm coat under the crystal chandelier in the General's foyer in Eaton Row. Her hair was shining and her skin was clear and she was six feet tall in these shoes; she saw herself as pretty and powerful, and she was sure he regarded her as smart and well-off and that he wanted to know her and to get rid of his awful wife. She imagined saying, "We'll turn heads" and saw herself entering the Ritz with him. Why were men so slow?

Women hate me, Lauren thought, sensing Mrs. Van Arkady's poisonous eyes on her. She believed that other women always envied and disliked her and saw her as a threat — it was one of her many satisfactions.

She knew she had left an impression on Van Arkady — she could see it in the General's mirrors — it was the perfect house to be seen in. But she left alone and walked to Victoria Station and took the tube back to her one-room flat. Tube was the perfect name for it at this time of night, and when she got back to her horrible flat she discovered her toilet was frozen solid. London!

2

The mink-lined coat was her own idea. "My own design," she said. But it was a simple design: a good plain Burberry with a fur lining — twenty-seven mink pelts that were hidden when the coat was buttoned up. It was the warmest coat she had ever owned.

Women who wore minks were showoffs, like her mother, who hadn't even needed it in Virginia. This mink lining had once been her mother's whole coat. A second-hand mink was a pardonable thing, but a new one was a crime. A black tailor named Noosie had carefully cut the old thing and fitted it into the new Burberry. Lauren did not pay the tailor, but later the sixty-two-year-old man took her to dinner — she regarded her agreeing to go as a kind of payment — and afterward in his room she allowed him to take photographs of her neck, from the front. That was Noosie's odd request. "More neck, darling," he kept saying.

She unfastened the top buttons of her blouse and sat straighter. She thought: Necko-philia! She wanted to laugh.

But he was very solemn; he was perspiring. His black face was beady-wet like a cold plum. He shot two rolls of film, stepping in a circle around her.

If he wants it I'll go the whole nine yards, Lauren thought. But when he was out of film he made her a cup of cocoa and walked her to the bus stop. She had prepared herself for something else, because she had wanted this useful two-sided coat.

She needed it in this freezing room. She hated the place, and she thought how unfair it was that she should go unrecognized. No one had yet seen how special she was: pretty, healthy, intelligent, well traveled — and she had style. She had no money — that was a bitch — but money was never hard to find. Yet brains and beauty and health! Did those women last night have any idea how foolish and empty they were, how ugly and neurotic, with a cigarette in one claw and a drink in the other? They coughed like outboard motors!

They hated her because she was young and, somehow, they knew she had been to China and was planning a trip to the Middle East. She could run a fast five miles, she was the first American woman Fellow at the Institute, she had once made love to her art history professor's wife. "I'm eclectic," she said. She had represented Culpeper in the Miss Virginia pageant at the State Fair. The professor's wife was an impulse — she had invited Lauren for coffee and touched her hair. Lauren had looked calmly into her eyes and seen a harmless lust, and she said what the woman was too afraid to say: "I want to scarf you," and did, there on the sofa, with the woman's dress pushed up around her waist and the woman tipped back and whimpering a little, as if she was giving birth. Lauren counted that afternoon as one of her accomplishments, because she was not sorry and she had not repeated it.

She did not deserve this Brixton bedsitter. It was heated by a small electric fire — two bars on a tin plate fixed to the sealed-up hearth, but it was unsafe and expensive to leave it burning. The day before she had stayed at the Institute and gone straight to the party and in those eighteen hours the toilet in the small cubicle in the hall had frozen. There was still ice in it now and frost on the black windows. London dampness was colder than any ice she had ever seen, and London ice was like dark stone — a kind of dirty swelling marble. Seeing the toilet she had said to herself, as if to a friend, "And I looked down and saw there was actually ice in the john!"

But she knew she would never tell anyone, which was a shame, because even though it was disgusting it was also very funny. It made a good story, but she knew she would have to be a success before she could tell it, otherwise she would be pitied.

Still in her mink coat she went into the hallway, where there was a pay phone. She found a likely number in the phone book and stood in her warm coat, dialing, and when Lindsay from upstairs passed by her and said, "All right?" she was pleased with herself, because underneath her coat she had nothing on, and he didn't know it. She enjoyed her terrific secret — standing there naked inside her coat.

"I'd like to speak to the plumber," she said, when the call

went through. Even on the phone she took pleasure in the half-truth of being naked inside her coat.

"Yeah, this is the plumber."

She was oddly encouraged by the stupid selfish tone of the man.

"The most incredible thing happened last night," she said, and took a breath. "My toilet turned to ice! I don't know what to do. I mean, what good is a frozen toilet?"

"You American?"

"I sure am," she said.

"I can't do anything before tomorrow," he said in a slightly friendlier tone.

"What about this evening," she said, "around Happy Hour — or whatever you people call cocktail time?"

He fell silent, but then he asked for her address and she knew he would come that evening.

"Coldharbour Lane," he said. "That's Brixton."

"Brixton is my new home," she said.

"What do you think of it?"

"Come on over and I'll tell you."

"Name?"

"Lauren Slaughter."

E ven that — her name — was half true. The gold initials on her briefcase said *L.S.* because it had been her husband's. Leonard Slaughter was English, and very serious. He taught economics at Hull. Hull was horrible! They had met in China and married in Washington and separated in London. They had China in common, and after they parted she saw his close-set eyes and big serious nose whenever she heard the word "China." And anything Chinese stirred memories of her marriage. It was this that influenced her in wanting to change her field of study to the Arab world.

Leonard had not wanted a divorce, but it was pointless to live the way they had been living, making a virtue of merely holding on. Leonard cared about appearances, which made him tenacious. Marriage was not a virtuous thing, only a balancing act, two people pedaling a tandem bike, one behind the other, the man in front. It was absurd and pleasant like that, and just as rare a success as in life — no, it was a short-distance thing and he steered and she pedaled. All marriage had done for her was give her a new name. Her old one was Mopsy Fairlight. She took the name Lauren when she got the name Slaughter. She wondered why people didn't change their names more often. She laughed and then concentrated hard when she saw her old name written on the flyleaf of some of her books — the words, the ink, the signature: where was this girl now?

Last night's dinner party had left her feeling rumpled and dissatisfied, as if she had been stupidly teased. In this mood she went to work. On the Victoria Line to Green Park and the Institute she repeated her sentence "When I feel like it" and she was pleased by the way it sounded. She liked her reflection in the train window. She was a young woman with a girl's face — the features almost of a child — but she was stronger than most men she knew; she could run faster and farther than they. Jogging at a certain speed, Leonard had always looked as if he was just going to fly apart.

At Stockwell a man got on and sat across the aisle from Lauren. He was a television director, or else an actor, or something in advertising. He was wearing lovely shoes — olive green, probably Italian — and he had nice narrow feet. He also wore a felt hat, innocently gangsterish. A young man who wore that kind of hat wanted to call attention to himself. He was dressed warmly — a Crombie overcoat with soft sleeves, and blue jeans. He was trying to look interesting and self-absorbed and he sat there comfortably with his *Guardian* still folded on his lap unread. Lauren found him sexy and self-assured — but for her they were almost the same thing. Something in his clothes and his manner suggested that he had been to the States. This she found attractive in him. She hated the housebound English.

She was peering past him, seeming to ignore him. But it was not shyness or lack of interest — she was looking at his reflection in the window and she wanted to give him a chance to look at her.

Then she made her move. She reached into her briefcase and took out *Renmin Ribao* — it was two months old, but how could he tell? She held it up and began reading busily.

"You read —" He smiled and pointed.

She smiled back at him over the top of the paper. "Chinese."

He had been quicker than most — seconds — but in that time she had actually found an article she had missed on other readings, and it was related to her new area — something about a Chinese trade delegation to the Persian Gulf. The Chinese were in the oil business, too, and had machinery to sell — this she gathered while the man waited for her to say something more.

He was not handsome but stylish — worldly, unattached, definitely not serious. He looked fun. He was something in television, she was sure.

Lauren folded the Chinese newspaper in half and held it out to him.

"Want to do the crossword?"

He laughed but took the paper and examined it and remarked what an amazing language it was. "You must be very clever."

She said, "On the other hand, I don't speak French and you probably do."

"You speak American," he said.

"Don't be cruel," she said, and tenderly touched his arm.

The train was drawing into Victoria.

"I hate this stop," she said. "All the commuters."

He shrugged and said, "I'm not going far."

She wanted to know how far, how long she would have with him, but instead of asking she made an amused face to show that she had not understood what he had just said.

"Oxford Circus," he said, in explanation.

"I'll join you."

He said he was a film editor for Olympus Pictures and that he had lived in the States for a year — New York. He then said, "Do you get back often?"

"Periodically."

He stared at her and repeated "periodically" — trying it out.

"You should go to Virginia sometime," she said. "But

there's no point going unless you have me to show you around."

He did not say anything in reply. He waited until the train drew into Oxford Circus and then, when the platform was clear, he said, "I'll keep that in mind. In the meantime, maybe we could discuss it over dinner."

The serious ones always said dinner. She had not expected this from him. His seriousness slightly oppressed her. They walked upstairs. She did not tell him that she had missed her stop for him.

"My name's Lauren."

"Ivan Shepherd."

At the top of the stairs she took a card out of her wallet. She liked handing over her printed card, with her new name and the two phone numbers and the Institute's embossed hemisphere — the world in gold. It was a ritual that made her feel important and protected.

"The Hemisphere Institute of International Studies," he said, reading from the card. He had no expression, he was thinking hard; he said, "You went past your stop."

"I have shopping to do," she said, and turned quickly and walked away while he was still gaping at her. And once she was out of sight she ran all the way to the Institute.

There was a seminar that morning on tensions in the Gulf. It was always tensions somewhere — the world was a wreck. This one concerned the war between Iran and Iraq, its effect on the Shatt-al-Arab waterway, but it was being held at London University over in Russell Square. Instead of going, Lauren spent the morning in the Institute library — an irritating morning, as it turned out, because the librarian would not allow her to use the photocopying machine.

"This is for staff use only," the woman said. "There's a coin-operated one on the third floor for the use of Institute Fellows."

Lauren said that Mr. Fletcher always let her use this machine.

The librarian said, "Then Mr. Fletcher is breaking the rules."

Mr. Fletcher was a lovely nervous little guy who lived with his mother; but this librarian was an insensitive woman with a chafed face and old brown shoes.

Julian returned from the seminar at one. When he was overworked he looked like an old man — round-shouldered and preoccupied and harmless.

"How about lunch?" Lauren said. "It's on me."

In the coffee shop on the south side of Berkeley Square, Julian said that the party had made him furious. He had spent the whole night wakeful, thinking angrily about the man who had said, "There are five thousand people in the world."

Lauren thought it was one of the brightest things she had heard in London so far — unless the man had been joking: she was still a little uneasy about that.

Julian said, "I wish I had said something scathing to him. I hate these people who are full of formulas and magic numbers."

"He was pretty incredible," Lauren said.

"He's a monster."

Lauren did not want to be drawn into a discussion of the man at the dinner — she was uncomfortable talking about things she wanted or people she liked.

"So how was the seminar?" she said.

Julian said that it had been poorly attended, and so they had been able to put a lot of questions to the people who had read papers. He described how the Arabs in the marshes of southern Iraq had been driven away, and their unique settlements which had lasted for thousands of years in this remote place were now destroyed by two trampling armies. The economy of Kuwait had been affected by the war, too. A man at the seminar named Haseeb was organizing a study tour of the Gulf.

"I'd love to go," Lauren said.

"You should have been at the seminar."

"I couldn't be bothered to go all the way to Blooms-bury."

"You're astonishing," he said, and looked Lauren over admiringly. "That's a splendid coat."

"I designed it," she said. "I design all my own dresses."

"My sister does that."

Lauren was irritated by his saying this. She said, "But I design everything. I'd design my own underwear, too, if I wore any, except I don't."

Julian seemed both shocked and grateful.

"I don't buy knickers," she said, playfully pursing her lips on the word. "Why do English people like that word so much?"

Julian said, "Because we're pathetic and repressed."

Lauren was pinching her empty purse and fussing with it, but before she could say, "I left all my money at the Institute," Julian said, "My treat," and insisted that lunch had been his idea, not hers.

"I hope you don't think I'm as coarse as this with everyone," she said. "It's just that I feel that I can relax with you."

"I'm glad. I'd like to see more of you."

"We can meet," she said. "Periodically."

He smiled at "periodically" as Ivan Shepherd had done.

"We can bitch about the Institute," she said.

"General Newhouse thinks your project is super."

"I'd like to stuff it to him," Lauren said. "I certainly never expected the head of the Institute to be a general. It feels like the army."

Julian said, "His war memoirs have been compared to *The Seven Pillars of Wisdom*."

"I've got a theory that it's very unlucky for a woman to read that book."

Julian smiled in a surrendering way, and she knew she had him.

"I think the General hates the research Fellows. I wish they'd get rid of him."

Julian said, "Americans come to a new situation and say, 'I don't like it. They'll have to change it.' "

"What do English people say?"

" 'I don't like it. Therefore, I'll have to change.' "

Lauren said, "I always think insecurity or a lack of confidence makes people susceptible to imitation. Weak people haven't got the guts to be themselves. But being yourself is being original! I like myself the way I am."

She found her face in the coffee shop mirror.

She said, "Still, he gives good parties."

"You only get invited to one. It's a sort of welcome."

"That's awful!" she said. "That's another reason I hate him."

She spent the afternoon trying to follow up the reference she had found in the Chinese newspaper, about the trade delegation from the People's Republic. She wondered whether Julian was telling the truth about the General — did he really think her project was super? "Recycling Oil Revenue" was her working title. Arabs were so much more cooperative than the Chinese, and the Gulf was nearer and sunnier and didn't smell of mud and smoke, as China did. She reminded herself that she did not hate the Chinese; but they irritated her — the thought of them, so many of them — and she smirked, remembering Mr. Van Arkady saying, "There are two people in China." She thought: Or one.

Alone, with no one watching her, she did not want to read. On the tube this morning with that young man across the aisle she had had no trouble concentrating on the *Renmin Ribao* — she'd had great concentration. Now she had none, and the English she was trying to read looked incomprehensible.

At five she saw General Newhouse leave. She put on her coat and followed him to the pavement, where a taxi was waiting.

"Is that your taxi, General?"

"Yes, can I give you a lift?"

They rode in silence toward Victoria. Lauren said, "Your party was fun. I really liked your friends."

The General stared at her, and then he said, "We were glad you were able to come."

She said, "We must do it again sometime."

He squinted at this, as if she had just lapsed into another language.

She said, "By the way, my research is going wonderfully." She wanted to mock his indifference by lying to him.

"I sometimes think that wealthy Arabs in London are the strangest phenomenon of our century. And someday they won't exist, and no one will understand how this happened in our time."

Lauren said, "Isn't there a reception for those Arab information people tonight?"

"I'm on my way there now," the General said. His face was set in a look of boredom. "It's by invitation, I'm afraid."

Lauren smiled, hating the creases in his face and the set of his mouth. She said, "Unfortunately I can't go — I've got a very important meeting."

Again, the General seemed to be having trouble translating her words.

They passed a shop on Victoria Street that had a sign that flashed SEX SHOW and LIVE ACTS.

The General pretended not to see.

"They're nothing," Lauren said. "I saw a sex show in Florida that would take five years off your life." Then she rapped on the driver's window and said, "I'm getting out here," and she did, without another word, leaving the General to pay.

The plumber was late and unapologetic. He looked suspicious and a bit amateur. He had no tools with him. He made Lauren feel like a crank and then she was afraid and sorry she had let him in. But when he saw the toilet he sighed and she was encouraged: now he understood. The ice had thawed to the size of a grapefruit, but it had cracked a pipe.

He said, "That'll need replacing."

What was he pointing at?

"Do whatever needs to be done."

"Who's the landlord here?"

"His name is Reggie. He's in Jamaica at the moment. But I can look after myself."

The man said something in a low voice. When they were saying something very rude you could never understand them.

He went outside and returned with a bag of tools — a heavy one: it thudded and rattled the windows when he dropped it. He was clumsy — banging, thumping, throwing things down. There was a kind of noisemaking that was a clear sign of stupidity in a man.

Lauren sat by the electric fire in the other room, still wearing her coat. The clatter from the hall turned to silence. The last noise was the toilet flushing.

"It's working," he said, stepping into the room.

"You're marvelous."

He hesitated. "Twenty-seven pounds," he said. "That includes parts and labor." He tore a sheet of paper from a pad — the bill. But she did not look at it.

She said, "Your parts?"

She went to a cupboard and poured a measure of whiskey. She gave it to him, she clinked glasses — hers was empty.

"Go on," she said. "I don't drink."

"This won't do you any harm," he said, and sipped, and his face tightened at the taste of it.

"You're a fast worker," she said.

"I reckon I am," he said, and sat down. He had begun to prowl.

"What's your name?"

"Pete."

"Sneaky Pete," she said. "Like another drink?" She took a step toward his chair. "I want to pay you." And took another step. "I mean, I want you to be satisfied."

He smiled sheepishly, as if he had been discovered naked, and then he grunted, and sipped the drink again. He was waiting for her to do all the work.

Lauren touched the back of his hand, and then moved sinuously around his chair.

"What are you doing?"

"The dirty boogie. That's what we used to call it." She knelt in front of him and said, "I think I know what you want." She unbuckled his belt. He did not object. "I want to please you."

He simply stared, and then he looked around and turned the lamp off. He did nothing more for a while. She fumbled with him, then held him tightly and used her tongue and her lips. She felt a sense of power, almost of magic — a kind of conjuring: she held this whole man in her mouth.

The man cried out, and then pushed himself back in the chair, as if slightly wounded — surprised by a burn.

Lauren stood up and switched on the lamp. She wiped a glistening fleck from her cheek, she straightened her dress; she had not removed her coat.

His trousers were down. He was limp, he looked weak and silly and unprotected. Lauren helped him to his feet and reminded him that his bag of tools was next to the chair. He looked at her in a shy amazed way, and then he laughed softly. He was pleased, and he had become grateful and boyish. All his rudeness was gone.

Lauren was holding the bill. She said, "Now you'll mark that 'paid,' won't you?"

When he was gone she did her exercises and the room felt warmer. She had a bath. She ate alone: yogurt, an apple, some walnuts, a slice of toasted wholemeal bread and peanut butter, and a cup of herb tea.

Another day — and in many respects it had been typical. For more than a month she had been living like this — on nothing — and hating it.

3

London was bad air and a sour mood, and on some days its clammy discomfort made her feel physically deformed; on other days she felt the city was poisoning her. But she was fighting it. She jogged down Acre Lane to Clapham and ran around the common listening to The Stranglers sing "Shah Shah a Go Go" on her Sony Walkman; then she jogged home and had a long bath; and then breakfast of tea and melon, and bran mixed with yogurt. Each thing — the run, the bath, the food — made her purer and stronger. She was reassured, knowing she could keep her health in this senile city.

She wanted to move out of Brixton — this black district made her feel like a failure. She wondered whether she should leave the city altogether. It would mean leaving Britain — it was London or nothing; but the only habitable part of London, as far as she could see, was Mayfair. A man at the party had asked her why she liked it — was it that Giles something from the Foreign Office or had it been Van Arkady? Anyway, she'd said, "It's really nice — it's just like Georgetown."

The rest of Britain was dreary, especially Hull, where Lenny — he hated to be called Lenny — still sat, trying to explain China to his students. Once they had gone to Cornwall. The English talked about Cornwall the way Americans spoke of California, but when she got to Padstow Lauren said, "Are we here?" There was no sun. It was wet and windy, and the sharp ugly rocks made swimming dangerous. She laughed in a hard shouting way when someone mentioned that King Arthur and Sir Lancelot had lived there. "And Confucius used to live in China!" she said.

Why were English rooms so cold? She had not been in a warm room once — a really warm room, where she could have taken off her clothes and padded around naked. When she grumbled or got sad about that she thought of "The Cremation of Sam McGee." She had recited it for the performing part of the Miss Virginia pageant, when she was Miss Culpeper. Miss Goochland played the clarinet but Miss Norfolk won with her roller skates. The Northern Lights had seen queer sights but the queerest they ever did see were those other finalists, and Lauren had looked at them and thought: You're all dogmeat.

She had begun to feel that same disgust in London and she now saw that it had been a mistake to skip yesterday's seminar. But she had had no way of knowing that a study tour to the Middle East was being set up. It would be a good way of leaving London and continuing her project.

At the moment she felt shut out and ignored and very cold — the jerks were sitting on her head, and the nice ones were no use at all. She wanted to drop everything and go to the Middle East: she imagined white skyscrapers and clean sand and blinding light. She had no money, but she could find some. The idea was to make a decision and then act. The money would come. She had never felt so left out, and that morning she went to the Institute determined to put things in order.

Julian was already in the office, reading at his desk. There were postgraduate fellows who, when they were studying, looked exactly like timid priests — sort of praying over their books. That was the way Julian folded his hands when he read. .

Lauren said, "I'm going on the tour."

Julian said he was surprised that she could be so confident of being selected. He pretended to be joking, but he was serious and sort of issuing a warning. He did not know whether he himself would be chosen. They were very fussy, he said.

"Then they're sure to want me," Lauren said.

T he organizer of the study tour, the man called Haseeb, was attached to the Kuwait Embassy. Lauren dialed the number that Julian had given her. She got a crossed line and a wrong number before it even rang, and then no one picked up the phone. She tried again nearer noon and got a busy signal. Ten minutes later a secretary said that Mr. Haseeb was out to lunch. Lauren thought: How can you get out without coming in? At three o'clock he had not returned; at four the number was busy again; at four-thirty he was in a meeting. And then no answer: the office was closed, and Lauren realized that she had spent the entire day unsuccessfully trying to make one lousy phone call.

The next day was Friday — no work for Muslims; but, being Arabs in London, they had Saturday and Sunday off, too. On Monday the secretary said that Mr. Haseeb was out of the office. What was that supposed to mean? Bosses turned their secretaries into liars and guard dogs. People like Haseeb yawned over a magazine and said, "Say I'm in a meeting."

Because of these frustrations — not being able to see or speak to the man who could help her — Lauren imagined Haseeb very clearly. He was a brown balding man with a warty face and big teeth, in an English suit, and he weighed two hundred and eighty pounds. He had to wear a special sort of orthopedic shoe because of his weight, and he had trouble getting out of most cars. He stank of cigarettes. He persecuted his huge wife.

On Tuesday the secretary told Lauren that Mr. Haseeb was away for the day.

He had hairy knuckles. His eyes were two different colors. There was dandruff on his collar.

"He's on holiday," the secretary said on Wednesday.

Eating like a pig, and sneaking alcohol. His farts sounded like air brakes.

Then Lauren could not work. In the week since she had made up her mind to go on the Middle East study tour Lauren had put her work aside, because she had been waiting. She could not think or even read a simple article when she was in suspense — it really was like hanging in the air.

"We'll send you an application," the secretary said on Thursday. Another Thursday and she was on the phone with the same question!

Lauren said, "I understand they're choosing the candidates next week."

"Mr. Haseeb didn't leave me any instructions."

"Would it speed things up if I came over and picked up the application in person?"

"Obviously."

The secretary said this word in that tone of voice because she thought she could get away with it.

"You just missed him," the secretary said when Lauren entered the foyer. Now she saw the secretary's name: Miss Humpage.

Lauren went to the window. The secretary was behind her, gloating — Lauren could feel the heat of it.

The young Arab getting into a black Jaguar wore a dark suit, and a tie like an orchid, and had the physique of a tennis player, and could not have been more than thirty. He looked back at the building and Lauren, who stepped nearer the window, put her hands on her hips and in this way opened her coat. But Haseeb had not seen her — couldn't possibly, or he would not have driven away.

The application called for an academic transcript, and — to satisfy the visa requirements of some of the countries on the tour's itinerary — it asked for a baptismal certificate, as well as a letter from the candidate's bank manager.

Lauren said, "How am I supposed to get a baptismal certificate?"

"In the usual way, one would think," Miss Humpage said, coldly. "By being baptized."

Did secretaries speak like this because of the awful people they worked for?

Lauren said, "It's bureaucratic and bigoted." Miss Humpage did not react. "It's very demeaning." Miss Humpage put a sheet of paper into the typewriter. "And it'll take months. Mine has to come from the States. And what's this about a letter from my bank?"

"Again, that is a visa requirement — we need proof that you have a balance of two hundred pounds in your account."

"Is that supposed to be a lot of money?"

"I wouldn't know," Miss Humpage said, lowering her tensed fingers to the keyboard.

"Then I'll tell you," Lauren said. "It's not."

Lauren was grinning, but she did not have this money in her bank account.

"I want to make an appointment with Mr. Haseeb."

Miss Humpage said, "Fill up this form. Just your name and a number where we can reach you. And your reason for the appointment."

Lauren did as she was directed, writing fast.

Miss Humpage said, "Is that a business or a home number?"

"It's the green phone," Lauren said.

Miss Humpage did not react. She read aloud, "To investigate the pattern of petrodollar investment —"

Lauren hated this, the woman reading at her from her own application.

"— by OPEC agencies in development projects —"

She spoke in a bored weary way, and at once the project seemed artificial and unnecessary. Miss Humpage looked up from the application.

"— in Third World Muslim states."

"And when Mr. Haseeb is sober and decides to show up, tell him to take that application and shove it up his ass — unless you'd rather do that for him, too."

On her way back to the Institute, and feeling frail, she entered a red telephone booth that was full of stinks and tried to call Mr. Van Arkady's bank. She spoke to his assistant. She heard the words "in a meeting" and knew it was untrue. What were these people really doing who said they were in a meeting?

The man said, "What is this in connection with?"

Lauren had called the number without knowing why, but the man's direct question made her realize that she wanted Mr. Van Arkady's help and friendship. He was confident and worldly wise; he had contacts; he had money. He would sit down and tell her exactly what to do. Now she hated being alone. In six weeks in London she had not made one friend, but she did not regard this man Van Arkady as a stranger.

"It's a personal matter. We're friends."

"I'll take your name and we'll get right back to you."

She said, "He doesn't know my name."

"Didn't you say you were friends?"

"Oh, yes. We are." Then she faltered. "Only I didn't get a chance to tell him my name."

After a silence, the man said, "I see."

"It's Mopsy Slaughter, but forget it."

Then she hung up.

I've got a feeling I'm not going on that study tour," she said to Julian later, in the smoky, noisy pub. It was almost six o'clock. Julian was drinking a pint of beer. Lauren had a glass of Malvern water. "I'd like to buy glasses of water," she had said and the barman thought she was mocking him.

Julian had a long withered sausage on a chipped plate. He seemed to regard it as a problem. He kept glancing at it but he did not touch it.

He said, "You don't need to go on the tour. You could probably find everything you need right here. Isn't that why you came to London?"

She said, "London isn't London."

"Ah, yes," Julian said in the self-mocking way that came so easily to him, "we are not what we were."

"Don't feel bad. Tokyo isn't Tokyo, and Peking certainly isn't Peking, and Moscow isn't Moscow. Singapore isn't Singapore either. But, Jesus, Calcutta really is Calcutta."

"I hope Berlin is Berlin," he said.

"Half of it is."

"I have to go there fairly soon to look into some archives on Arabia."

She said, "All you think about is work."

"What do you think about?"

"Don't laugh, but I think about my body," she said. "The really important things like running, eating, sleeping and washing. I mean, doing them right. Who gives a shit about our research? I'd rather run a marathon."

In his bewilderment at what she was saying Julian had overcome his nervousness with the sausage and had begun to eat it.

Lauren said, "How can you put that thing into your mouth?"

"I suppose it *is* pretty disgusting," he said.

She said, "Why doesn't the stupid General invite us to another goddamned party? I really hate him."

Julian watched her with the sausage sticking out of his mouth like a cigar, not biting down on it.

"Eat it and get it over with!" Lauren said. "You're driving me crazy with that thing."

When he was done and had wiped his hands she asked him for a loan of five pounds, which he gladly gave her.

The same evening of this long day Lauren was doing her stretching exercises on the floor when she heard Lindsay from upstairs shouting that a bloke wanted her on the telephone — English bloke, Cockney-like. Lindsay always gave information in a meddling way. He was from Barbados and always barefoot indoors and had wet glistening eyes. He studied karate.

"It's me — Pete." The voice was confident and casually familiar.

She said, "I don't know anyone by that name."

"The plumber." Then he cleared his throat. "Remember?" He cleared his throat again. "I did that job at your place."

She said, "You're the person who fixed my toilet."

"Yeah," he said. "Thought I might come over."

"I don't need a plumber."

"Thought you might like a drink."

She said, "I don't drink."

She heard him gumming and ungumming his lips.

"Thought maybe we could get together."

She said, "Sorry," and nothing more.

He became cross. "Well, what about the last time?"

"That was strictly business."

This silenced him. He tried again, but hungrily this time. "I want to see you."

She said, "I don't know you. You performed a job for me and I paid you. I don't owe you anything." And she hung up.

That phone call angered her, but she felt better after a bath, and then she sat in her mink-lined coat with the electric fire on, drying her hair. As the room warmed up old odors were stirred — food, sex, and dirt, all the human smells, the heat revealing the room's former tenants, the sour residue of their lives. London wasn't even pleasant when it was warm.

I t was Thursday once more. That was the awful thing about failure: it humiliated you again and again by repeating the same empty days. She thought: I should have done Sino-Soviet relations—

Chinese grants were easy these days — already people were sick of going to China. Then, remembering China, she saw Leonard's nose. Or the EEC, she thought: Paris was still Paris. She saw herself lecturing at a podium in Paris or Brussels, wearing her blue high-necked dress and white shoes. Then she thought: I would like to run a big hotel catering to the business traveler — he has special needs.

Julian entered the office from the library. He walked stiffly — he had been reading in his prayerful posture. Lauren knew that a mistake would be made and that he would be chosen by that little queer Haseeb to go on the study tour. She pitied Julian — he was wrong, incredibly naive, painfully truthful and timid, and always apologizing.

"Want a drink?" he said, in his embarrassed way, as if expecting her to say no.

She said, "When you offer me a drink you actually mean something to drink."

"Yes," he said.

"But with other people, yes to a drink means yes to everything. And why is it always a drink?"

Julian had begun to look hopeful.

He was rummaging in his briefcase. "This came for you this morning," he said, and handed her a rectangular parcel in a padded bag. "I signed for it. It came by messenger."

"Just a book."

"Okay then?" he said. "The Duke of York?"

She said no in a resigned way and went home in the dark leaving all her library books and her file of photocopies on her desk.

t was not a book. It was a book-shaped video recording. It had no label, and the parcel had no return address. She had a small black and white television set, but no video machine. Lindsay had one. He was a member of a Brixton video club; he rented pornographic videos, and ones about karate, and Nazi prison camps. His favorite was one called *I Spit on Your Grave:* rape and murder.

"Hello, stranger," Lindsay said. He was dressed like the kung fu hero on the poster near his bed.

She said, "I want to borrow your video machine. All that means is I want to borrow your video machine. Don't offer me a so-called drink."

"You're a really funny kid. I rate you."

Lindsay stood up. What was there about karate that attracted undersized people? Lauren took a step back.

"Just the machine," she said.

4

She watched the videotape in her room as she did her stretching exercises — naked, on a long straw mat, the blinds down, and the electric fire blazing and filling the room with dusty heat. Her exercises were like a dancer's warm-up — flexing her arms, and tugging one heel and then the other against her stomach, and finally salaaming slowly toward the television screen.

— *This young woman earns two hundred pounds an hour.*

The narrator spoke in a flat insulted voice and the film showed a woman hurrying through strolling groups of people in Park Lane. It was not a cheaply made film. It was a television documentary, well edited and with good sound — perhaps a BBC program that had been taped. The woman was seen from a number of angles, and Lauren noticed that she was very ordinary and overdressed, with podgy shoulders and a chubby chin and a big bum. Dog-meat.

— Her takings for a single week might be several thou-sand pounds —

"And she weighs three hundred pounds," Lauren said, stretching.

Now the woman was introducing herself to a swarthy mustached man who actually looked impressed and grate-ful — his libido on the boil and his tail wagging. The poor man was half the woman's size and he stood in his tiny Italian suit on stiff skinny legs.

— She is one of a growing number of young women who work in London's newest industry — the escort service —

His tone was interesting. It attempted stifled horror and distaste, but Lauren didn't believe it — she was sure the narrator was as fascinated as she was. With hidden cameras and bugged phones, the film progressed in a patchwork way, explaining the various girls-for-hire agencies that operated in Central London.

The girls looked unattractive and stupid — and they were certainly overpaid. Large sums were mentioned, but Lauren was still new enough to England to think of plain shapeless lumps whenever she heard the word "pounds."

— It's much more than they're worth, said a cherubic hooker in dark glasses. *That's why it's not prostitution!*

— I agree. This was a soft-voiced black woman with a vast shiny handbag. *Prostitution is lowering yourself like, but this is just the opposite.*

The customers seemed to Lauren unexpectedly young and well-off. The ones who were interviewed were excited at the prospect of meeting a girl. Most of the men were foreign, many were from the Middle East, a few were Americans. And an Englishman — but then Lauren remembered that this was England.

— *I like the simplicity of it,* one of the American men said. *I hate hassles.*

The man looked like Archie McComb from Culpeper — just as big and pleasant, the same beer belly, the same spiky hair. But this one had money.

— *Usually it's just a bite of something,* the man explained. *You get lonely. It's company. Sure, a bite of something and then you take a hike.*

It was apparently a discreet business — practically all the arrangements were made by telephone. The makers of the film stage-managed an appointment. The narrator's tone of voice prepared the viewer in a sarcastic way for a kind of viciousness; but Lauren found the operation reassuring and practical, if a little comic.

— *Jasmine Agency. May I help you?* The voice at the end of the line seemed trapped in a small bottle.

— *I'm ringing from the Hilton,* the man in the foreground said. Hyde Park was visible out the window. *I'd like an escort for the evening. For dinner and, um —*

— *Give us your name and room number and we'll ring you right back.*

— *Why is that necessary?*

— *It's just a precaution, sir.*

Of course, Lauren thought. The man gave the information and then put the phone down. When it rang again he resumed.

— *I'd like to know how much it costs.*

— One hundred pounds, plus twenty-five agency fee.
— What happens then?
*— The rest is by arrangement with the lady. Shall I
book an escort for you?*

The screen went black, the sound became echoey, and
now it was as if the cameraman was squashed behind a
door and squinting out. A doorbell rang loudly; there was
gabbling, and the indistinct motion of several humans, and
the friendly scrape of a Scottish voice.

— We don't take personal checks.

When this woman crossed in front of the camera Lauren
could see that she was expensively dressed, with an unnecessary and rather flashy scarf. But physically she was
very plain. She had freckles and fat knees and she was
definitely uneducated.

— Mind if I smoke? she said, lighting one.

Lauren laughed at the stupidity of it — the silly woman
stinking up the small hotel room with her cigarette, and
then coughing into her stubby fingers as she counted the
man's money.

— What did you say your name was?
— Samantha. Samantha Buckingham.

Lauren jeered at her. "Samantha Buckingham! I love
it!"

*— Pleased to meet you. I'm Frank Harris. I want to
take you to a party.*

— I like a good party, the woman said, and Lauren
smiled at the accent—how ignorant and ridiculous it was.

*— Then maybe later we can pop back here for a night-
cap. You don't mind that, do you?*

— Might cost you extra, depending on the time. Do you always talk this much? There's nothing to be nervy about, darling.

The next shot was of a party in the ballroom of a London hotel, a throng of shouting people — women in bright gowns and men in dark suits.

— Most of the women in this room are social escorts being paid anywhere from fifty to five hundred pounds to stand and smile. In some cases, rather more is required.

Their faces were crusted with make-up; they had gooey lips and lacquered piles of hair. Lauren saw mingled greed and gratitude in their eyes. And she thought they were pathetic — not for their lack of style or their silly sequined dresses, but for their heavy flesh and dull skin. They were hideously unhealthy.

The camera moved to a bright-eyed Arab at the party trying to speak to one of the girls and mumbling shyly.

— Here, what do you call that, then? the girl said, jerking the lower edge of his headdress.

"A ghotra," Lauren said.

— Ghotra, the man said. *It is for the sun and sand and windstorm.*

— Very useful in London that! The girl screamed with laughter.

Slob, Lauren thought; but the man was gently laughing with the girl.

— The Jasmine Agency has been operating for three years from its offices in Shepherd Market. Every evening of the year girls are dispatched to customers in London's hotels.

The narrator described the innocent-seeming premises of the Jasmine Agency, and its mysterious directors, as a small figure hurried out of the office door and approached a Daimler that had just drawn up to the curb.

— *This is Captain Twilley. He has been a farmer in Rhodesia and a sultan's bodyguard in the Persian Gulf. He has twice been arrested for firearms offenses — carrying an unlicensed revolver and being in possession of a stolen weapon. There is no record of his having earned the title "captain."*

A young and rather haggard woman emerged from the Daimler. Captain Twilley took her by the arm and escorted her to the door.

Madame Cybele. Her last known employer was the Hotel Bristol, Beirut, Lebanon, though her duties were somewhat obscure.

A reporter suddenly appeared in the foreground of this shot, startling the woman.

— *I have a few questions for you.*

The woman recovered and gave him a corrosive stare.

— *I cannot help you.*

Her voice was faintly foreign, and her slight accent and the overcorrect English made her seem all the more rude.

Captain Twilley loomed.

— *On your bike!* he shouted at the reporter.

The Captain had bushy eyebrows and a tweed tie and wore a thick baggy suit which had a bristly nap and a weave like sacking.

— *Certain aspects of your business seem rather strange to us.*

4 6

— *Stranger things happen at sea,* Captain Twilley said.

Madame Cybele's pale weary face was framed by a black fur collar. She had large eyes and large lips, and Lauren was interested to see that someone so young and attractive could also look so used up.

— *You will excuse us, please?* Madame Cybele said.

Captain Twilley shielded her and swept her into the offices of the Jasmine Agency.

This was not the end of the videotape. There were sequences of women at dances and dinner parties, and shopping in the West End — smiling at tiny watches on trays; they were shown at embassy functions, in restaurants, and at national day receptions under multicolored flags and banners. They were all paid for this.

Lauren was struck by how plain they were, how little conversation they had; their accents were uneducated and their health was mediocre; they had bad skin and wore too much make-up. They had heavy legs. They smoked. They were dogmeat.

She had stopped doing her exercises. She sat cross-legged, naked on the mat, still watching. And for the duration of the film London seemed a habitable city — it was human and workable. What had been incomprehensible to her before was now clear. She saw order: a pattern was revealed — motives and results, too, and for the first time something potentially friendly. The city no longer seemed foreign and half dead to her. She was thinking how much prettier and better she was than those women, and how powerful she could be. When the tape ended she felt invigorated with a peculiar strength. In this foreign place she saw something familiar and alive. And

the most important thing of all: in this huge city of
strangers someone knew her very well. It was the person
who had sent the tape, and Lauren felt that this person
— he or she — was still whispering encouragement to her.

Lauren tried on her Thai silk dress, pale yellow
with bright stripes, and her Italian shoes —
two narrow straps and a three-inch heel that was so sharp
it jammed in escalators. Her shoulders were bare, her hair
upswept, and her thickest gold chain round her neck —
Noosie, the Brixton neck freak, had drawn it tight and
photographed the welt it had left. Now Lauren posed in
front of her full-length mirror and smiled: Party time! She
had worn this dress to a cocktail party at the Hemisphere
Institute and to General Newhouse's dinner party. She
knew that as a political economist she was disconcerting
in it, and she loved the tactical advantage in being disconcerting.

This dress would not do — it wasn't right. When she
took it off, the rustle of silk and the sight of her own
nakedness aroused her. She felt queenly. Then she parted
her legs and teased herself with one fingertip and she
shuddered with pleasure at the white length of her body.

She put on a dark tartan kilt, and a white pleated shirt
that she buttoned to her neck. She drew on her oatmeal
tweed jacket.

She said, "I think this recession can be explained by a
credulous overdependency on supply-side theory."

She fastened her grandmother's brooch onto her lapel
and turned back to the mirror.

"On the other hand, in China until very recently all external debts were settled immediately in cash, taking no notice at all of the float possibilities."

She tugged her hair back and wound it and fixed it with an old tortoiseshell clasp — her "librarian clasp"; and she glanced again at the mirror.

"Petrodollars are definitely bottoming out. If they hit the tape at one-twenty your oil producers may begin to sell gold."

She pulled on her boots and stood up and stamped in them.

"As seen from Mayfair, the downside risk is lethal but worth taking."

And last she put on a pair of gold-rimmed glasses.

"I'm now a virgin," she said. "You break it — you pay for it."

It was ten o'clock in the morning. At one, a Fellows' Meeting was scheduled in the Situation Room of the Institute — cheap wine and cheese sandwiches and a pep talk from the General. There was time, there was time.

The videotape had suggested sumptuous offices by showing a plaster façade painted in the dead white of a Nash terrace and with ornate grillework, and the sort of pompous brass nameplate that the Institute itself had mounted over its porcelain doorbell. This one said JASMINE AGENCY.

Lauren rang and entered — as a smaller notice demanded — but instead of stepping into comfortable space and warm light she found herself at the bottom of a steep flight of stairs. And it was chilly, too — like being at the bottom of a well.

On the landing high above her were two men in robes, snatching at their heads in frustration. It was an Arab gesture that looked like a frenzied benediction. They were speaking to a receptionist, who was seated at a small desk with her morning paper and her cup of tea. Lauren had expected to see Madame Cybele at the top of the stairs and she was disappointed by the girl at the desk — another bulgy bitch, like the ones in the program.

Each of the men — she now clearly saw that they were Arabs — wore an English suit jacket over his white robe. They were jabbering in a hurt, puzzled way. The language barrier so often made foreigners look stubborn or childish — it was what Lauren hated most about having to speak other languages: she felt infantile saying "Please" and "Thank you" and "Very good" and all that talk in the present tense, like a silly novel trying to look brisk and important.

Lauren shut the front door and the men stopped talking as the door slam reached them. Now they looked down the steep stairwell at Lauren rising.

"Hi!" she said. She was smiling and even after that long climb she was not winded.

The men backed away as if to receive her, and one blinked in satisfaction and said, "We want this one."

I t was the first time she had ever been early for a Fellows' Meeting. She sat primly, waiting for the others. They entered self-consciously, heaving briefcases and not speaking — Julian, Fairman from the Asia Section, Stringer, Willymot, and Brigid Doyle, an affected girl ("ashoom" she said instead of "assume") with broken teeth who rode an old bike and never took off her greasy raincoat. Apart from Julian, they all hated Lauren: Fairman because she had been to Chengdu, Willymot because she had stuck him with a restaurant bill their first week, Stringer because she had borrowed his cheap fountain pen and lost it; and Doyle — obvious.

Julian whispered, "Any luck with your application?"

"What application?"

"Haseeb," he said. "That Kuwaiti chap. The study tour."

This delighted her. She had completely forgotten all that. She said, "Fuck it!"

Julian pinched his face. He did not understand.

She said, "Don't care!"

The General entered and addressed them in a tone that was both bullying and patronizing, speaking of their research projects (fat Brigid was doing famine relief!). What Lauren hated most about his tone was that it showed no trust in them, no interest, only a sort of vague irritation that these research Fellows existed; and, all the while he spoke, he wore the expression of a man who hears a mosquito buzzing but can't see the creature he is impatient to swat.

"Finally," he said in the little homily he always saved for last, "the Arab world. A word. I don't have to tell you that it's on our own doorstep. I know some of you" — he looked at Lauren — "have met with a certain resistance. Don't be discouraged and above all don't be foolishly suspicious or wrong-headed. Your efforts will be considerable but so will your rewards. The Institute's relationship with the Arab world has grown out of an unprejudiced enthusiasm for the land and its peoples, and should any of you decide to pursue your researches further it would give the Institute a tremendous strategic advantage in applying for gifts from Arab agencies trading in the UK —"

The two men had taken her to the coffee shop of the Hilton and bought her a cup of espresso and a large piece of Black Forest gâteau. They took her protests for friendly excitement, and she said no so vigorously they ordered her a second piece of cake. She broke the first cake apart in a ceremonial way, to show she was grateful; but she did not taste it, nor did she drink the coffee. When she ate even a tiny morsel of something she didn't like she could taste it for two days.

Each of the men ate a slice of baklava, and then one wiped his mouth on his handkerchief and said, "We go?" to Lauren.

They left the other man at the table grinning at his wristwatch. He had shown Lauren the watch. Its face was a solid gold ingot weighing fifteen grams. He had also, that same morning, bought a large stuffed bear and an air pistol. The teddy bear was for his wife, he said tenderly, and he was going to shoot birds with the air pistol. There were many birds in his country — many, many birds to shoot at. He was still yapping about bird shooting when his heavier friend swallowed and said, "We go?"

"What's in the bag?" she asked.

He whisked it open as if at a Customs check.

"A book!" she said. "What's the title?"

An Arab with a book: it half scared her.

"No, no," he was saying, and pulled it out. He lifted one of the hard covers and plinking music began, the first few bars of "The Floral Dance," but even a few bars was enough to get this man wagging his head happily.

"Ah, that's better — a music box," Lauren said. "A book is a pain in the ass, isn't it?"

The man was still wagging his head to *pinka-pink, pinka-pink.*

She could never tell the ages of foreigners. This man might have been thirty or forty, or more — she believed that middle age was a certain musty soapy odor, and he had it on him. He gave her a hundred pounds in twenties from a canvas money belt that looked as if it held slugs of ammo. Then he went to the bathroom and washed noisily, and he stood by while Lauren washed, supervising her in a fussy way that had nothing to do with sex. When she lay naked on the bed, he knelt between her legs and lifted his robe. He had not taken it off even to wash. His penis was thick and dark and looked like an old pickle. He entered her, pushing hard, and only minutes later he ground his teeth, and cried, "Khallas!" and was done.

She was washing, using the bidet, when the second man slipped into the room. She had left the bathroom door open in order to keep an eye on her handbag, and then she saw this second man come toward her to watch. And the hotel room door slammed: that was the first man leaving. They had it all worked out!

Without speaking, this man took a socklike purse from his pocket and a plug of bills from the purse. When she had finished washing herself, he handed it over. Lauren took five long strides to the bed and tumbled in. The man

5 3

peeled off his skullcap and massaged his shaven head as he contemplated her. Something was wrong — he seemed distracted, at once modest and impatient. She reached for him but he drew back, keeping his hands from her, as if fearing contamination. Then he shuffled toward her and gave her a little slap on her hip — an animal pat. It was an order. She understood and turned on her stomach.

"Take it easy," she said, facing the headboard and seeing his dim reflection in the varnished wood.

But he had started with his finger and already it hurt. He was lost in a gabbling monologue with himself, and using her hipbones as handles he shoved himself into her abruptly, surprising her.

The swiftness and the slight pain made Lauren sob, which seemed to please the man. He pushed in deeply and rode her and then lay the length of her with his teeth clamped on her neck and squealing softly like a sudden rabbit.

"Any questions?" she heard the General saying.

She frowned, remembering, then said, "No, sir."

She had agreed to meet Captain Twilley at the Jasmine Agency that evening. The videotape was still so fresh in her mind that she felt as if she was part of the same film — but a vast improvement over those tacky English girls and that fat Scot who had coughed as she counted her money.

Captain Twilley was much smaller in the flesh and very gruff.

54

He said, "Escorts don't normally come to the agency, so don't make a habit of it. Use the telephone instead. We'll keep track of your appointments and send you a weekly invoice. That's all I need from you — your name and your telephone number. Your real name. We guarantee absolute discretion. If you want to use another name for work, that's fine. We don't ask awkward questions. This is like the Foreign Legion."

"I want to use my real name."

"That's very unusual."

She said, "I'm not ashamed of what I'm doing."

Until that moment he had been scribbling on a pad and only glancing at her. But now he looked up and kept his eyes on her as he leaned back in his chair.

"You're a bright spark," he said. "But I'm less than ecstatic about your outfit." He spun one finger in a winding motion that he intended as criticism. "Have you got anything a little more colorful that would emphasize your figure?"

"If you think a social escort is just tits and a tight dress you have a very old-fashioned idea of what this job requires," Lauren said.

"What have you got that it requires?" he asked.

She said, "I'm user-friendly."

"Good," Captain Twilley said. "We get all kinds of punters."

The next night she was summoned to the Savoy by a tall French boy, eighteen at most, who greeted her in his room wearing a red baseball hat with limp cloth horns — like cow horns — sewn to its crown. Their meal was sent up. He ate in his underwear, the hat on his head. She peeled an orange and ate three segments. They watched television. He kept his money in a paper bag. "Tarzans," he said, stirring the ten-pound notes. "Tarzans." He paid her and then went to sleep with his head in her lap. He woke and wept when she said she had to go home, and then he screamed and frightened her, and slammed the door as she walked quickly down the corridor.

She felt wonderful afterward, as if she had walked a tightrope and won the grand prize. Her only regret was that she had to go all the way to Brixton to be home. She wanted something nearer — a flat in Mayfair — perhaps a short distance from the Institute; she wanted her two lives separated by a few streets.

That same week she was sent an invitation to a reception at the Dorchester. It was to welcome a delegation from the Bahrain Ministry of Information. The minister himself was there, and so was the ambassador. The invitation had been delivered to the Institute by a messenger, and it was only when Lauren saw Captain Twilley waiting in the lobby that she was sure that she was representing the Jasmine Agency and not the Hemisphere Institute.

Captain Twilley took her upstairs and into the ballroom by a side door, bypassing the receiving line and a beefy-faced Englishman with side-whiskers and a red frockcoat who was shouting the names of the arriving guests.

"Look for Puddles," Captain Twilley said, and hurried downstairs for another of his girls.

Lauren saw Madame Cybele approaching.

"Puddles?"

The woman's frown meant yes. But Lauren thought: if

someone's called Puddles you don't ask why. Lauren liked
Madame Cybele's dark eyes and cruel fleshy mouth, but
something else disturbed her. The high collar of her dress
did not quite hide a gray bruise on her neck — the top of
the splotch just showed. This bruise, there, seemed to
Lauren very decadent — what was it about necks that
made men crazy?

"Follow me," Madame Cybele said, and she snaked
through the room. It was mostly men, and nearly all of
them Arabs — in *besht* and *thobe* and red-flecked *ghotra*,
like a desert gathering; and others in suits, and in various
military uniforms. They were unusual clothes and made
the party seem festive, like a fancy dress ball: these men
dressed as Arab sheiks and those as potentates and those as
stage generals. Most of the men looked wealthy, and they
had bad posture, as if they did nothing but sit or ride or
be carried.

Madame Cybele stopped at a group of three men. Now
she raised her voice and became charming. "Gentlemen,
I'd like you to meet a young friend of mine."

Each man smiled and spoke his name quickly, like a
sentence in Arabic.

"They're very generous, but ever so naughty," Madame
Cybele said, in an affected way that did not go with her
intelligent eyes or her bruise. "Be very careful, Lauren,
they're from Kuwait."

"I wonder whether you can tell me," Lauren said to the
men, "what effect the Iran-Iraq war has had on the tribal
people living in those immense marshes north of Basra and
the Shatt-al-Arab waterway. I mean, the Madan and the
Faraigat."

The men stared at her, and then one spoke.

"Very trouble," he said and put on a sorrowful expression.

Another said, "Yes, too much trouble for them. But I am living in Bahrain today."

"He keeps inviting me there," Madame Cybele said. "One of these days I'm going to surprise you and say yes."

But Lauren was still closely attentive. She said to this man, "I have great admiration for your pipeline."

"Well, well," Madame Cybele said.

"Awali to Dharan," Lauren said.

"You'll excuse me," Madame Cybele said, a trifle coldly, and slipped away.

"And Sitrah. And Jebel ad Dukhan," the man said. "You know Zahran." He showed Lauren his foot. "I buy this shoes in Zahran. This is the most expensive shoes in the world."

"I hope you've got two of them," Lauren said. "Then you can show me around the Gulf and not get sore feet."

"Please visit Kuwait," the third man said. He had been watching with bright squirrel-like eyes, and smiling each time Lauren spoke. He was intelligent looking and had a good accent — none of this "Very trouble" or "zis shiss." He was chafing a small string of worry beads in his fingers.

"Nice beads," she said.

"Moqaddimeh." And he pressed them into her hand.

They were heavy and cool — perhaps jade, perhaps something even more precious. The clasp was gold. She smiled, feeling powerful again, because without any effort she was a success; and what could they possibly deny her when she was trying hard to please them — she knew that she had an unusual capacity to please men. It had everything to do with forgetting her own pleasure and being a willing slave.

"I wanted to go to Kuwait," she said, handling the beads in her long fingers. "But Haseeb at your embassy flatly refused to see me."

"I have no embassy," the man said.

"But you know Haseeb!" one of the other men said. "Haseeb is just a small boy. And a lazy boy. I will arrange your visit. No Murphy's Law, no very trouble."

"What do you think?" Lauren said to the man who had given her his worry beads.

"I think you should come with me," he said, "so that we can discuss this" — and he smiled — "at the highest possible level."

He pinched the tip of her elbow and steered her toward the door. Then he released her and hurried forward to embrace someone — another man. They kissed and greeted each other with great formality — murmuring; but whether it was English or Arabic she could not tell.

"Meet my friend."

Who was being introduced — she or the man? Then it didn't matter. The man was Hugo Van Arkady.

At the General's he had seemed swarthy and heavy; in this gathering he looked thinner and rather pale and intense. But it was merely the difference in the setting, she was sure. He registered no surprise at seeing her.

"We've met," Van Arkady said. "And I was sure that we would meet again. You're keeping good company, Dr. Slaughter. Don't let this man's enthusiasm discourage you."

She said, "You remembered my name!" She was pleased,

for why would he bother to remember her name if he did not think she was one of his special number? It was magic more than memory: she was suddenly part of the city, and now everything in London seemed possible. That was an important moment for her — his easy assumption of friendship and her delight. And he didn't judge her, nor did he seem to care whether she was an escort or a research Fellow. It was as if he had known her for a long time — that, rather than the other way around, because she also found him a little scary looking, and if she had not felt like a success she suspected that she might be afraid of him, as she had been — slightly — at the General's.

"We must make arrangements," the man said.

Van Arkady said, "You both look very happy. It is wonderful to see you — wonderful."

In the nightclub the man said his name was Karim and that he hoped they would meet again soon. He said, "I know what you want."

She said, "I want you."

"That is a great deal," he said. "But if it makes you happy" — and he made a face at her at the dark and candlelit table.

"That man Van Arkady is an old friend of mine," she said.

"Oh, yes," he said. "I could see."

"But there's nothing to be jealous of," she said.

Karim nodded gravely at this and then ordered a feast of lamb and chicken kebabs, with a great bowl of rice, and lemon soup.

Lauren did not eat anything. Karim picked at one kebab, but when he murmured that Lauren really ought to eat something — it was good, a traditional feast, it made you strong and lovely — when he said this, Lauren grasped a skewer.

"There's something sexy about these," she said. "The way it's raw where the skewer pierces the meat. I love these skewers. I even like the word 'skewers.'"

These skewers were swords. Karim presented her with one, wiping it on his napkin and telling her to take it home.

"But why?" she said.

"Because you are my chicken."

5

In the daytime there was the Institute, and at night the agency, but she found the work similar in many respects; and when people (day or night) asked her what she did the rest of the time she said, "Research," and she thought: I've gone the whole nine yards.

She saw Karim often. It was always business. He said she should get a flat in London — he innocently believed that Brixton was not in London.

"I'd love a place in Mayfair. Halfway —"

She was going to say "Halfway between the Institute and Park Lane," but she forced herself to be silent. She wanted to keep her two lives separate — she was superstitious in a routine way, and she was also practical. And she had succeeded in dividing her life: at the Institute she let everyone know that her real name was Mopsy, and they called her Mopsy; at the Jasmine Agency, and to most of the men she was sent to, she was Dr. Slaughter — it was

Van Arkady's greeting that had given her the idea.
"Cheerio, Mopsy!" Julian said at the Duke of York, and
an hour later she would be speaking into a house phone
at a hotel: "This is Dr. Slaughter. I'm in the lobby —"

"Halfway," Karim was saying, urging her to finish her
sentence.

"Halfway through Mayfair."

"Yes, yes, yes."

He was glad in the way that wealthy men became glad:
she had never seen this in anyone else. These men had
everything they wanted — they had so much that they
could not imagine what someone else might want. They
could grant any wish, and yet they lived in a rather
saturated world in which people seldom expressed a wish.
It was maddening for them, and that was why Lauren's
saying "I'd love a place in Mayfair" made Karim grateful.

A few days later he took her to a small flat on Half
Moon Street, at the Piccadilly end, number three. Here
he photographed her as she sat naked in clear plastic chairs
or as she pedaled a Finnish exercise cycle. He took his
pleasure that way, talking to her the whole time.

"Is this yours?"

The question embarrassed him: he was still taking
pictures.

"The flat," she said.

"You like it, don't you?"

She said, "You know what I want."

"Yes, Doctor."

"You're an awful pimp," she said.

She was just teasing, but he didn't laugh.

She thought a moment, still pedaling as Karim knelt

with his camera, and she said, "There are a lot of things I
don't have. But I'm not greedy. I don't want a car. I'd
rather have my own room and the freedom to do anything
I want in it. I don't want to be bossed around. If there's
one question I hate it's "Where have you been, young
lady?" I don't care much about jewelry. I don't care
about the things I'm being denied now. I want the things
I was denied when I was twelve years old."

There was as yet not much furniture in the flat on Half
Moon Street, but even so she became attached to it, and
she disliked having to leave it and take the tube to Brixton.
These days Karim always used the flat, photographing her
and talking. Was this sex? If so, it was the oddest slowest
kind. Sometimes he took an hour or two. That was the
trouble with the kinky ones — they needed time. The
others were different. She prided herself on being able to
blow an average guy and be at the door in fifteen minutes,
shaking hands — that was always how they wanted it —
and leaving. She was never kissed. Karim did not even
touch her.

He shared her with his friends; they were bad and boring, but no worse than husbands — and they paid. She
agreed to it because there was no jealousy, because it was
business, and because with Karim's friends she was allowed
to use the flat on Half Moon Street.

Often with these men there was no sex, but instead long
noisy nights — too much food, and too much talk; and
back in Brixton she fasted and exercised. The men were a
useless combination of wealth and laziness, but they were
so kind. They were always exposed, always waiting, always self-conscious and they always gave her too much

money. She always felt she had the advantage. She still called it dating.

Some others were American — businessmen: they would answer the phone while she licked at them. "I'm a little tied up at the moment — I'll get right back to you." So many of them were vain about their hair, and one put on a rubber bathing cap before he got into bed with her. Another one told her in explicit detail how she was to take him into her mouth, and then he added sharply, "But don't touch my hair." They wore gold chains and expensive pendants around their necks. When they were violent or very stupid Lauren said, "I've got to get up real early tomorrow!" and left quickly. If they protested at this, she said angrily, "Don't you treat me like a hooker!" London was full of vulgar brainless bitches who would do anything for a weekend in Spain or a new pair of boots, but how many of these bitches had a master's in economics and a doctorate in international relations?

"I've just flown in from Hong Kong."

"I've been there," she said.

"I closed a pretty big deal." They were both cautious and boastful.

She said, "When I was in Hong Kong I was using the archives at the university. They've got some fantastic stuff on the People's Republic."

But the men could be pathetic.

"My name's Lauren — what's yours?"

"Anthony J. Pistorino," one man said.

He swallowed and blinked, because it was a lie — an hour later he forgot the name; but whenever she remembered it she laughed.

Another thing about the men was that they were seldom young. And when it was late and they were tired they looked older; their fatigue gave them a grief-stricken expression. Lord Bulbeck was like that — sorrowful eyes at midnight. He was well known for his charity work and in his flat he kept photographs of himself receiving awards for his efforts. One night as Lauren was leaving Lord Bulbeck's flat in Queen's Gate, she paused and peered at a photograph. The foot of some airplane steps: Lord B. hugging a white-haired man.

"He was a very important man."

She said, "Really?"

"A very great statesman," he said, as if to a tame little whore.

Lauren said, "Ben-Gurion, yes. That whole issue makes me feel very left wing. But, before you say he was greatly misunderstood, I will tiptoe away."

Lord Bulbeck looked up, amazed that she knew the face.

She decided that he was a lonely man. He said he had no friends now and often did not feel safe. That was why he had gone to the Jasmine Agency, and that was also why — after the first few times — he would not accept anyone but Lauren. One evening he took her to dinner at Claridge's. He was celebrating, he said. "I'm seventy years old today."

She said, "I'm flattered that you included me."

"There is no one else."

Then she wanted to justify herself and give him a little encouragement, too. She said, "I've got a Ph.D., you know. In international relations. You didn't invite a dummy to your birthday party."

He said, "I know all about you. A man with my views has to take great precautions."

"What sort of views?"

"The sort that are not changed by discussion," he said, and that was that.

When he paid the bill he said, "As a boy I used to walk past and see that man out front dressed in his fine uniform — his top hat and gold braid. I wanted so badly for him to tip his hat to me, and open the door. 'Good evening, my lord.' "

"But that's exactly what he did to you tonight."

"Yes," Lord Bulbeck said.

She said, "I know just what you mean."

He shook his head. He smiled at her, because it was too much trouble for him to explain. He began, saying, "My father sold scrap iron in Limehouse. I was always a Labour man," and then he gave up, though she knew that he was only trying to tell her that he had been made a Life Peer in one of the Honours Lists — did he really think an American wouldn't understand a simple thing like that?

She went home with him. She said, "One of these days I'm going to take you to my place on Half Moon Street."

"In the meantime, let us make do with a tango at Queen's Gate."

Was it tango or tangle? Anyway, that was what he called it. She liked the way he talked. He said, "Another bottoo of wine?" He said, "Peepoo can be horriboo."

These old men still had life left in them! They were slow to get started but could go on for ages. Lord Bulbeck always said, "I've been planning this for days." But another old man paid her double the rate to give her enemas.

He too had come through the agency. It made her wonder about security. But then she discovered an answer of sorts. She asked another girl at the party. "Arabella" — they all had assumed names like that — just laughed.

"Security? Don't be silly — whatever for?"

They were so stupid! Lauren wanted to say, "Don't you know that you're an incredible security risk?"

But they didn't know — so they weren't. Their stupidity was a form of security. And only Lauren knew that she needed a baptismal certificate and a bank statement and her grandmother's maiden name on an application to go to some of these countries — but she could take all her clothes off and sit on the ambassador's face on the recommendation of Captain Twilley or Puddles.

She knew that Captain Twilley found her cold.

He said, "Karim likes you" or "Lord Bulbeck wants you back" in a disbelieving way, and sometimes — not obscenely but with genuine curiosity — "What have you *got?*"

"An education," Lauren said. She did not like the man. He talked too much about the army.

He said, "It doesn't take an education to get fucked."

"No one fucks me," she said, staring back at him. "I do all the fucking. It used to annoy me, but now it suits me fine."

She guessed that Captain Twilley must have told this to Madame Cybele — Lauren still could not bear to say the word "Puddles." The young pale woman invited her out for a drink and mentioned it: Lauren liked her big soft lips and idly imagined kissing and biting them. This was at the Ritz, both women drinking Perrier (four pounds for two glasses of water, but it was a lovely place) and Madame Cybele repeated Lauren's remark. It had been polished by the retelling and had the sound of a "saying."

Lauren said, "I was thinking of Karim and his cameras. And that flat of his on Half Moon Street. Have you ever seen it?"

"He doesn't live on Half Moon Street," Madame Cybele said.

"His studio, let's say," Lauren said. "I'd give anything to live there."

"Don't ever say 'I'd give anything.' It can be dangerous." Madame Cybele looked at her from across the table. "I know. I got here the hard way."

Lauren said, "That sounds awful."

Madame Cybele seemed to read the questions in Lauren's eyes. She said disgustedly, "The things they say to you!"

Lauren said, "I hate the ones who don't wash."

Madame Cybele shrugged. Why was it that her bruises never quite vanished, but lingered as faded inky stains on her very white skin?

Lauren liked her for saying then, "They never think about a woman's pleasure."

"All they ever want to do is bum me," Lauren said. "I always come home feeling like I've been riding a bike — they're killing my ass."

Madame Cybele smiled — it was the first time Lauren had ever seen her do so, and Lauren was encouraged to ask her the question that had remained unanswered for weeks.

"Did you ever send me a videotape?"

"No." But Madame Cybele became watchful.

"That's why I looked you up that first day. It was a program about escort agencies. Yours was in it."

"I know. It was a stupid program."

"So who could have sent it to me?"

Madame Cybele stood up and kissed her and said, "Be very careful." Lauren returned the kiss tenderly and felt the young woman's frail body beneath her winter coat, like a bird's bones under its feathers.

Usually, she was glad that she seldom saw Madame Cybele, and she avoided Captain Twilley. And the girls she saw at parties were too busy hustling to talk. She was alone. She preferred it this way. She regarded herself as a success, both at the agency and at the Institute.

"I've got so much work to do," she said. But she only went through the motions; she never intended to finish. What was the point? Being an escort had calmed her and made her undemanding at the Institute; and her wide reading had made her a sought-after companion. Now Captain Twilley was polite when he called to give her an appointment, and General Newhouse spoke of extending her fellowship.

She wrote a paper on the possibilities of a banking crisis precipitated by the overproduction of oil and consequent price-cutting. Her emphasis in the paper was on the economies of Third World countries and their defaulting on debts. The arguments were hers, but Julian had helped her substantiate them by turning over to her all his notes. Afterward, the General said, "One word, Miss Slaughter." It was never "Mopsy" or "Doctor." "I think that theme is well worth pursuing for publication, but you desperately need documentation." She remembered this, because within the next half hour a man she had never seen before was kneeling against her and saying, "Lauren, put this in your mouth."

The time came for the study group to leave for their tour of the Gulf. Julian said, "We'll miss you."

"Send me a postcard."

He misunderstood. He said, "If it was any other year, I'm sure you'd be going instead of me."

That was the sort of gentle, dumb remark he made.

Lauren had more than three thousand pounds, cash, stuffed in the coffeepot she never used. She had standing invitations in Kuwait, Bahrain and Qatar. Lord Bulbeck had a regular date with her on Wednesdays and once he had said, "I don't know what to do about my will. There's my flat, my books, and all my furniture — I shall do whatever you tell me." She had had a long discussion with the editor of *Arabia Today* ("Pretty much the same as yesterday," she had said when he told her his paper's name; but she had proven her seriousness by asking about the Sunni-Shia split). "Anthony J. Pistorino" had wanted to take her to Geneva for a week. Karim was always saying, "Use my driver." She believed that she could have anything she wanted.

She said sweetly to Julian, "One of these days I might get lucky and go. Tell me all about it. But be careful in Kuwait. You'll go in a tight end and come out a wide receiver."

He inclined his head at her.

"It's a football expression."

He said, "Not English football."

The day Julian and the others left Lauren met a man named Shafique at Half Moon Street — one of Karim's friends, though when she mentioned Karim the man denied that he knew him, and he mysteriously said, "Who do you work for?"

"Myself," she said.

One day Ivan Shepherd called the Institute and asked Lauren to dinner. It seemed odd being called "Lauren" here, but she looked at her appointment book and said yes — tomorrow — and what was the name of his hotel?

He said, "Ivan Shepherd — don't you remember me?"

"Yes," she said, "a long time ago on the subway!"

"Six weeks ago on the tube," he said. "How about it?"

"I'm really much too busy these days," she said; but she wanted to say, *You've got to be joking!*

"Busy doing what?"

Instead of replying she said, "Hey, did you ever send me anything in the mail?"

"No," he said, and repeated, "Busy doing what?"

"Having dinner, actually," and hung up before he heard her laugh at his presumption, for even if he meant dinner — and he probably didn't — he would be getting free what a grateful man would pay two hundred pounds for.

That was the usual price and they *were* grateful, too, because when she said, "I want to give you pleasure," she meant it.

The paradox that particular day, when Ivan Shepherd invited her for dinner — why did men always mention food when they meant fucking? — that same day, Roger, the assistant librarian, saw her in the Reference Section and squeezed her breast as if he was honking a horn and she said, "That *hurt!*" He said, "If you tell anyone, I'll kill you," and looked crazily at her.

Also, that same day — this was why she gave up her diary, because there was too much — Karim sent her to visit one of his Kuwaiti friends and the man spent the whole evening drinking tea and earnestly describing de-salinization schemes.

It was not sex so much as safety these men looked for. Most of them were wealthy men whom this big foreign city turned into bewildered boys. They knew very little about life in London. They had never heard of Brixton, they thought that a hundred pounds for two in a restau-rant was about right, and they were afraid of the dark. They knew nothing.

Lauren said, "A girlfriend of mine's toilet froze over a few months ago."

"No." The man was German. This was at the Inn-on-the-Park. They were in his room watching a pornographic video in which a toilet figured.

He said, "Your friend was lying to you. It is not cold enough. In Hamburg, yes. In London, no."

"That's what she said. She never lies."

"Impossible."

It made her feel like a heroine; it made her hate her room. She smiled, determined to move out.

"You like it, *ja?*" The German was pleased. He thought she was smiling at the man and the woman and the toilet.

The following Wednesday she told Lord Bulbeck that she was looking for a place to rent in Mayfair. "Or Queen's Gate?" he said, suggesting that she might want to move in with him; but she was not ready for that. He said he would look around. Some days passed and then, impatiently, she asked the agency to get in touch with him — that was the procedure: a girl could not telephone a client directly. Lord Bulbeck phoned her and said he would gladly find her a flat — and he would pay the rent. "You don't understand," she said, but then he rang off saying a motion was being proposed. She tried him twice through the agency, and twice he returned her call: he had one or two leads, he said.

The second time Lauren signaled that she wanted to get in touch with Lord Bulbeck, Madame Cybele said, "I shouldn't say this to you, but you are being very stupid."

Lauren said, "You're right. You shouldn't say that to me."

And then she had her wish. Karim took her to the flat on Half Moon Street — to photograph her, she thought. But, no: he toured the three rooms with her. There were cushions and carpets where there had been bare floors, and the room with the clear plastic chairs and the Finnish exercise bike now had plants and bright curtains.

Karim said, "It's yours. I know the landlord. He needs someone reliable like you. An academic person."

Of course — because it was people like Roger who treated her like a hooker. *The only person who ever assaulted me and threatened me with murder was an assistant librarian.*

Karim brought her the papers; she signed, she paid, she got the keys and a one-year lease. And she moved into the top-floor flat on Half Moon Street, number three.

The street itself was nothing — a narrow connection to Piccadilly, the backs of buildings, a small hotel, some black railings, the pale smooth pillars of the Naval and Military Club. But the flat was special, and it made her so happy that when she thought of herself in it, or saw herself in a mirror there (she had always liked the suddenness and the teasing glamour of mirrors: there were five big ones here), she felt important and beautiful and very proud. The first thing she wanted to do at Half Moon Street was call Hugo Van Arkady and say, "Come over for drinks some evening." That meant everything. She also wanted to call Lord Bulbeck and treat the good old boy to a free night — it would mean a lot to him. But she couldn't call either man: agency rules. She didn't complain — this isolation as an escort left her free to go to the Institute. And in any case one day soon Lord Bulbeck, and probably Van Arkady, would call her and come to the flat and say, "Ah, you've arrived!"

Half Moon Street was at the very center of things. She had found the middle of London. And the most remarkable thing about the flat was that though Lauren was often alone in it she was never lonely. That was the test of all property and that was the measure of her happiness on Half Moon Street. It was everything she wanted, and she found her solitude delicious.

She had left Brixton without telling anyone. She had wanted to vanish without a trace — those very words occurred to her. What did Brixton know of Mayfair? This was the London she had always imagined herself in, and as with many people whose fondest wish is granted she felt very healthy, and stronger than ever. She slept soundly. She became very conscientious about her food. Long ago she had banned salt, white sugar, milk, cream and anything with preservatives. Now she banned what she called animal products — no meat at all, not even chicken bouillon cubes. She ate fresh fruit and steamed vegetables, brown rice, lentils, roasted nuts, mushrooms and yogurt. She tried to include half a cup of bran a day. She made stock from potato peel, she drank herbal tea and bottled water, and after a run she had honey on wholemeal toast. Her weakness was for peanut butter. "I do one of these a week," she told Rahman — one of Karim's friends — holding up a jar of Harrods' peanut butter. Occasionally, she ate fish — poached or broiled, but never fried. "Like the Hindus say, fish are a kind of sea vegetable."

She ran without stopping entirely around the edge of Hyde Park every morning, clockwise from Hyde Park Corner to Kensington, then north to Bayswater Road and along it to Marble Arch, and down the broad walk parallel to Park Lane. It was seven miles. After a shower — she had four showers a day but only shampooed her hair once — she went to the Institute: library in the mornings, an apple and a piece of cheddar for lunch, and conferences or a seminar in the afternoon. The place was unusually quiet — nearly all the Fellows had gone on the study tour to the Gulf, even Brigid, who was supposed to be doing starvation somewhere else, and Fairman the Asia man. Willymot was upstairs counting nuclear warheads, but she never saw him. In the evening after her stretching and a spell on the exercise bike she took agency calls.

It was surprising how many of her dates — she hated Captain Twilley's calling them "punters" — were interested in eating right. Not Arabs, of course — they stuck to traditional food and were (as well as being generous) the most inflexible and narrow-minded people she had ever known. But Americans, Germans, and all the Scandinavian people liked talking about what Lauren called the dynamics of diet. The sex was predictable — with Karim's friends it was always perfunctory and nearly always bumming; and everyone else wanted to be sucked off. So much for the varieties of sexual experience in Western civilization! Yet it made life simple and she was glad of that.

But afterward at the late supper she never ate she often talked about food.

"These tomatoes are very bad for you," she said. "They're full of acid. Potato skins are good roughage and loaded with vitamins, and there's a lot of goodness in these snow peas — unless they boiled them. People are always boiling the goodness out of things. But stay away from these dumplings and that gravy. I always think sausages are just plain destructive. I'm a salad person —"

She could tell how civilized a man was by his willingness to listen to reason about his diet. Savages were the real junk food freaks, and drinkers and smokers too. She hated smokers so much she refused to kiss them — it was the only line she drew — but kissing in the traditional way was the rarest act she performed. They hugged her and squashed their hands on her; they pushed her head down. But she didn't object. Her power was in making them feel powerful, and sex often made her feel like a ravishing witch, for after they had come they were small and weak, and they would need her again to make them strong: the crude magic worked. She said, "Fuck my face," and helped them struggle, and when they were done she swallowed and said, "It's good, you know — it's all protein."

She considered writing a paper on diet and health, using Lévi-Strauss's studies of Indian culture and food as a model for Arabia. She wanted to look at high blood pressure and heart disease among the super rich in the oil-producing countries. And what about gastric ulcers and respiratory ailments — all that drinking and smoking by simple desert people? But General Newhouse said no. It was not that sort of institute.

"Unless you plan to publish your findings in *The Lancet* I suggest you carry on with your study of the recycling of oil revenues. What a pity you weren't chosen for that study tour."

She told Karim that she wanted to talk to Van Arkady. She wanted the victory of his visiting her on Half Moon Street.

Karim said, "He is very busy. He can't speak to you."

"Is his bank connected with your embassy in any way?"

"In a way, yes," he said, challenging her with a smile, "because I have no embassy."

"You're being mysterious again."

"Because you are asking improper questions," he said. "Now take your clothes off, my darling. Do you mind?"

"Why should I mind?" And she laughed as she flung them off. Karim was so generous. He had found her this flat, he had given her most of the furniture and that

Finnish exercise cycle and a leather chair from Barkers and a Lalique panther made of lead crystal from Harrods. "But I hate your friend Latif. He's a bully."

"What does he do?"

Karim was using a large gunlike camera — making a videotape of her pedaling the bike.

She said, "He spits in my mouth."

"Lift your knees a bit higher, darling."

She was not posing but really pedaling for the sake of the film. She said, "This is great exercise!"

"Stop smiling," he said. "What about Rahman."

"I always confuse him with Raheem."

"But Raheem is the hungry one."

"How do you know that?" and turned around to face him.

Karim said, "Keep pedaling."

"Yeah," she said. "He bites me. Sometimes he leaves marks, and I have to wear my track suit to hide them. Some of your friends are real animals."

"Perhaps only with you," he said.

She said, "That's very true. Only I know what they're really like."

Karim said, "Go on."

"Forget it," she said. "Rahman gave me some perfume. Tina Farina. In a limited-edition bottle."

Karim said, "I don't leave marks," over the whirr of his camera.

But Lauren was thinking of that terrible German and his toilet movies, and the man who made her put on rubber underwear ("I don't even wear the normal kind!" she complained), and the Spaniard who commanded, "You must give me a black kiss. Do you know what is a black kiss?"

That was what they were really like: they had small hot secrets.

She said, "There's no sex anymore."

Karim had stopped listening. His camera was whirring. He said, "Pedal harder!"

This sex: a virgin could do it and remain a virgin. It was virginal sex, or rather, not sex at all. It was service: she did not feel violated. She was asked to cooperate or perform; to see or be seen. The men groped across her body, some did not touch her at all but merely watched her use her fingers on herself. Often, nothing but her attendance was required — at a banquet or a party. She was once in the same room as the Duke of Edinburgh. The rest was physical, and some of it high school stuff, but it was not sex — not fucking anyhow — and though it frequently confused her it left her feeling pure. Now she understood Madame Cybele's distraction, and those bruises on the young woman's white skin.

When a man asked for more time all he wanted was time. At dinner he might say, "I want you for breakfast, too," but he would then spend the rest of the night snoring beside her in his king-sized bed, or else showing her off to his friends — towing her in and out of rooms for them to admire. So greedy, so eager, so puny! Most of them had nothing but money, which seemed to Lauren like the cruelest form of destitution. They overreached themselves, these men, in sex as in their business lives. Their loneliness made them unreasonable. But usually they just submerged themselves in sleep.

All that was required of her was tact — don't mention the uneaten meal, the sudden sleep, the unused and useless portion of the jeroboam of champagne; not a word about the hopeless fumble and apology, that bump in the night: "Sorry, I don't think — oh, never mind —" She wanted to say "You don't have to apologize, darling." They were demanding by nature, but in the circumstances in which she saw them they were children. She wanted to say: *Your eyes are bigger than your — et cetera!* They made her feel like third helpings. And there she lay until they woke up blinking at her pretty face and honey-blonde hair.

Often they wanted no more than her companionship. One man, a superstitious Portuguese — banking — spent hours showing her his good luck charms, and they included a shrunken head — a hard hairy prune with sewn-up lips. A man from Needles, California, who was working on an oil rig in the North Sea had a gold belt buckle engraved IF YOU AIN'T OILFIELD YOU AIN'T SHIT. With such men it wasn't sex. It was that they did not want to be left alone and lonesome in this wet winter-dark city. Sometimes it was just like a sink.

This particular man asked for a weekend. He said his name was Guy, and Lauren knew he wasn't lying — Guy was not the kind of name you made up.

"What did you have in mind?"

Once a man had said: *What kind of knickers — ?*

"Nothing special," Guy said.

For a weekend! But really it was just the sort of vagueness she expected for this length of time. He was like the rest of them, except that he was being honest.

She said, "A weekend's a long time."

"In the country it passes quite quickly," he said. He sounded cute and nervous. "We'll be staying with friends. It's all arranged."

He picked her up late Friday afternoon at the Institute in his Triumph. He was young, about twenty-eight — but some of these English people could look much older than they were, wearing incredibly ugly clothes and with terrible posture, and there were thirty-year-olds in London who had gray hair. Guy was surprisingly good-looking and probably played tennis — he certainly didn't smoke. He walked on the balls of his feet in a tennis player's way. Now Lauren was glad it was going to be a weekend.

The agency fee for this was three hundred pounds. Lauren considered asking only another three hundred, she liked him so much, but she didn't want him to think she was a hooker, so she decided on an even thousand. She kept the price to herself for the moment.

He said, "I love finishing work on a Friday and leaving London. It's like breaking out of jail."

He drove too fast — over seventy: the English were so childish about speed, and the other Europeans were worse, French and Italians especially. But at least he kept both hands on the wheel.

They were on the Great West Road and had now passed the suburbs of semidetached houses, the vegetable fields farther on, the airport. Now it was dark, and just the occasional scatter of lighted windows far off the road indicated a town or a village. Occasionally, a sign saying WALES or OXFORD flew at them from the darkness ahead.

His dog woke up and began barking. Lauren had taken the thing for a hairy blanket in the jump seat. She felt his damp nose at the back of her ear and something else against her hair — perhaps his jowls or his flapping tongue. He stopped barking, he slurped at the side of her head; and she smiled, remembering much worse men.

Guy said, "Get down, you stupid dog!" and the animal retreated.

"He doesn't bother me," Lauren said.

"He thinks he's a person, that's his problem. He's really neurotic. He prevents me from having anything like a worthwhile relationship with anyone else. He gets jealous."

Lauren was enjoying the solitary pleasure of smiling in the dark. She had not been this happy for months. Yes, she thought. They never had animals, and they were never so young, and never so relaxed. Guy was an unusual fellow. He wasn't shifty or apologetic. I could even stand the dog, she thought. She saw herself walking the beast in Hyde Park on Sunday mornings and buying newspapers at the corner and bringing them back to Guy. He wasn't like any of the others. This weekend was going to be fun.

"What's his name?"

"Him? Shmuel."

"What's it mean?"

"It means he's a special sort of mutt, like me."

Lauren said, "I think you are pretty special." When he laughed at this she added, "I think I am, too," and he stopped laughing.

Answering one of her direct questions, Guy said that he worked at a merchant bank. He startled Lauren by saying, "I have a rather lowly position at the moment, but if I get a transfer I'll move up a few grades. I've put in for Hong Kong."

Lauren said, "There's much more money in the Gulf. Dubai, for example, would be perfect. I've been to Hong Kong — so I know. The Gulf is my field now."

Guy said, "The Gulf might be awkward for me."

"Not if you want to do business," she said. "You should

see the profiles of some of these Gulf banks. Megabucks!"
There was not much light on Guy's face, but he seemed
to be smiling and nodding in agreement. She said, "I bet
we've got a lot in common."

Why didn't he say something?

She said, "We could meet there. It might be fun traveling together."

He smiled again, but was staring straight ahead at the
empty road. Finally he said softly, "I'm sure you know
much more than I do about the Gulf."

"Want to know a secret?" Lauren said, but she had already started to laugh. "I don't know shit about the Gulf!
I chose it because it's the opposite of China — that was my
husband's big thing. But the Gulf — God, I don't know
the difference between emirates and interest rates, and
I'm supposed to be able to talk Gulf economics! Hey, I'm
just sucking my thumb."

Guy's expression did not change. He was still smiling
in a studious way at the tunnel his headlights made on the
road ahead. Lauren wondered whether she was boring
him.

She said, "I don't know why I told you that," and
frowned. "Maybe it's because I've never told anyone
else."

He said, "You've got a husband."

"*Had* a husband." He had missed the point — seized on
the most unimportant detail.

"And China!" he said.

He really had missed the point by a mile. She said,
"You've never been there or else you wouldn't be so wild
about Hong Kong. China's just boring and depressing,

but Hong Kong is worse in a different way — if it was human you'd say it was tasteless, spoiled, overweight and had high blood pressure. When the lease expires in 1997 the PRC is going to take over and kick the shit out of it. People are already leaving — and you want to go there!"

He said, "You know these places intimately, of course."

"Sure. My Chinese work got me the Hemisphere fellowship."

"What about your escort work?"

"It's not work."

He said nothing. It was an English habit not to hit the ball back. You sometimes had to serve again and again.

"I'm flexible," she said.

He kept driving.

"I can fit anything in," she said.

Maybe he hated himself for being with her.

"I live alone, so most of my evenings are free."

He said, "So you're not seeing anyone at the moment."

She laughed. "I'm seeing a lot of people! But not steadily. Do you know what I mean by a sex partner?"

"Approximately. Have you got one?"

"Not at the moment."

"And yet," Guy said, "something tells me you've got your hands full."

She said, "You'd be surprised how much I can handle."

He chose not to reply — well, what could he say? And he was concentrating on his driving. They drove off the motorway onto a dark twisting road, walled by thick hedges which showed in the headlights.

Lauren meanwhile had been reflecting in a hopeful way,

and now her mind was made up. She said, "I'm sure it would work out."

"Sorry?"

"You and me," she said. "In the Gulf. Dubai, for example. A kind of working vacation at first. I'm sure we've both got a lot of contacts there. We could just play it by ear and share expenses — see how we get along. It might be fun."

He said, "I put in for Hong Kong, but even if I tried to get a transfer to the Gulf it might not go through for another year." He sniggered in a self-deprecating way and added, "I don't fancy my chances."

"You'd get it easily!"

"You don't know a thing about me," he said, almost sternly.

Then Lauren realized that she had gone too far, planned too much — she was always skipping ahead. But she had been dealing with rich successful men; she wasn't used to young struggling executives who called themselves middle management and were anxious for a one-rung promotion.

"It's not far," Guy said. "Just a few more miles."

Lauren said, "You don't have to apologize, darling."

He had been there before — she could tell by the way he raced up the driveway, taking the two curves fast and scattering pebbles as he braked before the stone canopy at the front door. Lauren was saying, "Hi!" to the old man approaching the car, but Guy said nothing, only gave the man the key to his trunk, and then Lauren realized she was warmly greeting the butler — the servant anyhow — babbling at him. She was embarrassed but decided to make a democratic virtue of the gaffe and kept talking to the old man as he heaved the bags at the door.

She sensed something like hostility in the man — fear and anger — he was trying to drive her off and save himself, because how could he explain to his employer — the woman who was walking slowly toward Lauren — that this American girl had insisted on chatting with him?

"Guy!" the woman cried and lifted her hands to his face. She was tall and bony and sure of herself. She wore a shapeless gray suit and had white streaks in her hair. But Lauren saw that she was not more than thirty-five or so — she had young skin and lovely hands.

"And this is your young lady," the woman said, turning to Lauren. "You must be the lovely Julia."

"I'm not," Lauren said. "Does this mean I have to go back home?"

Guy said, "Maura, this is —"

"Dr. Slaughter," Lauren said, putting her hand out. "But you can call me Lauren."

The woman did not take her hand, and so Lauren stood there feeling like someone who had just dropped something.

Maura said, "I'd much rather call you Dr. Slaughter."

Lauren said, "If it'll make you feel better."

Maura was still speaking. "Like someone in Trollope."

They had been walking quickly as they spoke and were now past the hall and approaching a long room where two men and another woman were sitting before a fireplace.

The men got to their feet as Maura entered with Guy and Lauren.

"I always like a little Trollope in bed before I go to sleep," one of the men said and smiled at Lauren.

"So does Sam," the other man said.

"Wasn't it Harold Macmillan who said that?"

"Surely it was Lennox Berkeley?"

Lauren saw that each person in the room was sneaking glances at her and, as they knew Guy, probably sizing her up. Was she good for him? Were they serious? Did she have anything to offer? Did she have a nice figure? You silly fucks, she thought.

The other woman, introduced to her as Sidney, asked — apropos of what? — "Are you interested in music, Dr. Slaughter?"

She said, "I like playing the mouth organ."

"Do you know English music?"

"I think it's tremendously underrated — particularly in America," Lauren said.

"There!" Maura said.

"The Stranglers are way ahead of their time," Lauren said. "They're practically geniuses."

"You're a very brave girl." Was that man smiling?

Sidney said, "I'm not familiar with The Stranglers, I'm afraid."

" 'Shah Shah a Go Go'? 'Baroque Bordello'? 'Walking on the beaches, looking at the peaches'? 'Rattus Norvegicus'?"

Lauren stared at them as she spoke.

"Slaughter," the woman named Sidney said in a thoughtful way. "Don't I know your father from Nairobi?"

Maura said, "I'll show you upstairs."

They had separate rooms, she and Guy, and not even adjoining ones.

Lauren said, "Is this going to work out?"

"Perfectly."

"You'll need a map!"

But she wanted to say, *I hope these people aren't good friends of yours, because I sort of hate them.* Instead she said nothing; she liked Guy too much to embarrass him. She saw that he was a few years younger than she and she wanted him more: *My young husband . . .*

She knew they were trying to mock her, but she did not know whether they were succeeding — and that was maddening. They were certainly telling private jokes, which was a way of ignoring her; but were they ridiculing her?

"Americans put such extraordinary things on their feet," Maura said, after Lauren and Guy returned to the long room.

They kept saying things like that. But this time Lauren decided not to let it pass.

She said, "Every time I see an Englishman I think, What's that stuff on his head?"

She felt their gaze on her.

She said, "And it's usually hair."

Alan — Maura's husband — said, "You're new in London, I take it."

"Sort of. I could have had Peking, but I'd been there before. I figured I'd try London and if it didn't work out I'd look at my options."

"I understand," Maura said. "She said to herself, 'I'll suck it and see.' That's very American."

Did they know something?

Alan said, "I can't think what's keeping Sam."

Guy said, "He's probably speaking. You know Sam."

"Yes," the woman named Sidney said. "He's a very passionate man in actual fact, isn't he?"

"On certain subjects," Guy said.

More private jokes, Lauren thought: mock the guest by keeping her in the dark. She had an urge to say: *There was a girl named Roberta Wiljanen at my school who had six toes —*

"Your young lady must be ravenous."

No, just bored stiff — and she hated to be spoken about in the third person: the big English thing. She said, "I'm not hungry at all. I had an apple, some walnuts and plain yogurt just before I left London."

Maura, suspecting, looked annoyed.

"Vegetarian," Lauren said, and beamed.

She had kicked off her shoes. They looked at her feet.

Maura said, "There's roast beef for dinner."

"I'll just have a little salad."

"Perhaps we can organize an omelette for you."

Lauren let disgust flicker across her face. "In some ways eggs are worse than meat."

"Now I never knew that!" the second man said. His name was George — "Geo," the others called him. He seemed fascinated by what Lauren had said, but it was all show. He turned abruptly to Maura and said, "Next week at this time you'll be in Les Houches."

"Aren't you going this year?"

"Been," he said. "But we're through with Chamonix." He smacked his lips and said, "Val-d'Isère. Fabulous. Powder. Three thousand meters. Scared Sidney rigid."

Guy said, "I was at Mégève over Christmas."

"Was it fabulous?" Maura asked. "I've heard Mégève's heaven."

Guy said, "I think I marginally prefer Klosters. Greta Garbo lives there, but so what?"

They were off, they kept talking, and they had turned their backs on Lauren. No one addressed a word to her, and it took her some minutes of listening to work out that they were talking about skiing. From this conversation she was totally excluded — she wondered whether it had something to do with her having blurted out that she was a vegetarian. God, she had enjoyed telling them that. It always wrong-footed a hostess when you saved that for the last minute.

She hated this skiing business — people they knew, places they'd been, heaven, fabulous, exquisite food. It was all incredibly boring, just a recitation of names, because how could you discuss skiing except to say that one place was good and another was lousy? It was stupid and the proof was, would anyone talk this way about swimming? And it was the same kind of thing.

But the worst of it was that Lauren had never been skiing.

"I'm told that Les Arcs is really superb. We didn't book in time. You fly to Geneva and take a coach. The *pistes* run right up to the hotel apparently."

Should she say that she had skied but had given it up

after a serious leg injury; or still skied every year in Aspen — yes, we have lots of skiing right in Colorado; or should she mock the whole idea of it and say that it was like talking about swimming? But no one asked her. The conversation did not come her way. She didn't count. And when Guy became solicitous and asked her in a whisper whether he could get her another glass of Malvern water she began to dislike him and to wish that she had never come.

They're really and truly awful, she thought, and she grew a little sentimental thinking about the busy breathless man she would be with tonight; she thought of Karim, and of Lord Bulbeck, and their loneliness. She had liked Guy on his own, and she hoped it would be like that again upstairs.

"I much prefer the food at the French resorts."

They were still talking about skiing!

"Bumpy gave me a new pair of boots for Christmas," Alan said.

"I got a really chic anorak," Sidney said. "And matching salopettes."

Anorak? Salopettes? Lauren wanted to laugh at them.

Perhaps they noticed her smiling, because Maura said, "Do you ski?"

"Periodically."

Then an alert listening look brightened Maura's face. Lauren had seen that look before on other people — it was a house owner hearing the sound of someone in the driveway. It was inaudible to everyone else; you had to own the house to hear it.

"That must be Sam."

Maura went into the hallway and after a suspended silence she shouted at her guest and there was a commotion — stamping feet, the banging of a suitcase, a loud kiss, a slammed door.

"He's here —"

And now the men were calling across the long room, and bantering, "We'd just about given you up, Sam," because the guest was so late, and in this chatter Guy said, "Hello, Uncle."

Lauren was thinking: Another one. And since they all pretended to be old-fashioned here she decided to keep her back turned and go on toasting her toes until they got around to introducing her. She sat with the cat on her lap, thinking about skiing, how she had never gone. But you couldn't do everything.

Now the guest was in the room, treading the carpet.

Guy smiled with a kind of insistence at Lauren — he wanted her to get up and greet his uncle. His uncle! England was all relatives!

"And this is Dr. Slaughter," Maura was saying. "She is rather preoccupied at the moment with our cat, Rudy. Perhaps she is a vet? Dr. Slaughter, I'd like you to meet Lord Bulbeck."

She turned quickly and saw that he was smiling. He shook her hand and said, "Pleased to meet you, my dear."

She could not see either affection or anger in his smile, and feeling off balance she looked for Guy. He was talking with Sidney, the younger of the two women, who was so self-assured with her big knockers, pretending she didn't see them swinging. Guy looked interested and responsive, that flirtatious energy, that nervous thirst, and Sidney was enjoying his discomfort and turning her headlights on him. Guy was different now from the circumspect young man who had driven her up from London. If Lord Bulbeck had not been there she would have taken Guy aside and whispered, "I'm going to sneak into your room upstairs and eat you."

But Lord Bulbeck was still smiling vaguely at her, with a kind of forced politeness. And, when Maura told him she was off to Les Houches, he said, "I know it's not an originoo thought, but the French have no principoos."

"That was a very flattering profile of you in *The Times* last week," Geo said.

"I don't find it flattering when journalists refer to my nose as bowbus."

"I meant your part in those Middle East peace talks."

"I'm just an errand boy," Lord Bulbeck said.

He had the floor. When he spoke everyone listened.

He said, "It's a horriboo errand."

Lauren loved the way he talked, his little bubble-blower's mouth puckered under his fat nose: *originoo . . . principoo . . . bowbus . . . horriboo.* And she was sorry that he was probably mad at her for finding her here with someone else. But that was tough luck for him: everyone paid, which was why she was free.

The hostess seated Lord Bulbeck next to herself and separated Lauren from Guy, so that Lauren was stuck with Geo, the middle-aged man who said, "I came to ski-ing rather late," and then began boasting, in his English way, at what frightful risks he took and how bad he was.

For Lauren, all dinners were very long: it was her being a vegetarian that made this so — she knew; and as a nondrinker she found most parties interminable. Her only diversion was in seeing how carnivores and boozers underwent a personality change as they crammed the junk into their mouths. Meat-eaters grew tired in an animalistic way — did they know how long it took flesh to be digested? — and drinkers just got crazier. Now, after the meal, everyone was clumsier and louder, sort of stumbling like squinting zoo monkeys after their feed. Lauren almost ran from the dining room when it was over — she hadn't exercised all day: that was the trouble — but Lord Bulbeck headed her off, and before the others overtook them he said, "You're looking well."

"I hope you're not mad," she said. "I never met these people before. I came with Guy."

"Of course —"

"You probably want to kill me. But I didn't know he was your nephew."

"If he wasn't you wouldn't be here," Lord Bulbeck said. "And neither would I."

"I don't get it."

"I'll explain everything later," he said. "Upstairs."

She said, "I'm a Fellow at the Hemisphere Institute," because the others had entered the room.

He said, "You're a lovely fellow!"

But upstairs, after midnight, Lord Bulbeck did not explain anything. He came to her room and in his big soft funny-uncle way he held her and told her how beautiful she was.

She said, "So it was a trap."

"I know all about traps," he said. "People try to trap me often enough."

"But it's a pretty roundabout way of getting me into bed," she said.

"Very roundabout, very safe."

She said, "Think how safe it would be in France."

"Frants," he said. So he found her pronunciation funny, too!

She said, "I want to go skiing, Sam."

"Anything you want, ducky, but please don't call me Sam at breakfast."

It was a perfect weekend. She was two people, and it worked so well she had at times glimpses of a third — the person she believed in and trusted. On Sunday evening she drove back to London with Guy, and neither said a single word.

7

They had traveled in the same plane to Geneva; but in different sections — Lord Bulbeck flew under the name Green in first class and Lauren was Mopsy Fairlight (it was an old passport) in tourist. They went through Customs at the same time; but Lord Bulbeck was waved along by an official and he was picked up by a Mercedes flying a United Nations flag, while Lauren took a taxi. They were both staying at the Holiday Inn, but in separate rooms. And yet at midnight they were together — in his room — and again he marveled at her beauty.

"You Americans are so big and healthy." He spoke with gratitude and even humility. He said, "I'm so lucky to know you. I feel puny and old."

"That's why you don't want us to be seen together."

"That's not the principoo reason."

She laughed hard, and she laughed again when he said the word "genitoos."

"You'll be real healthy after the skiing," she said.

"We shall see."

That was their first night in Geneva, which seemed to her an uglier and duller place than shoreline Chicago, which it somewhat resembled — Chicago with mountains. Lord Bulbeck told her that his committee would keep him there for a few days and that he would follow her to the resort.

"You're going tomorrow," he said. "Get an early start. The car's coming for you at eight. It's a four-hour drive to Bourg-St.-Maurice, and I'm told the hotel is on an impossiboo road at eighteen hundred meters."

"You have to promise on the Bible to be there."

"The Byboo is not my book," he said. "But I promise."

Lauren left him in the dark early morning and went to her room to pack. The driver was young and very silent, but she saw his eyes in the rearview mirror; and she was reminded of a taxi driver in London, who took her back to Brixton and demanded nine pounds because it was after midnight, and she had said, "Come upstairs — wouldn't you rather be paid there?" and she had done him in a few minutes and sent him down exhausted. That was fun, but that was before. She thought: I'll only do it for fun again, and if I want it.

They crossed drearily into France on wet gritty streets which continued for miles, and then to Annecy where the snow was coated with a black lacework of soot. The lake was an improvement, and soon the light was better and they were in sight of high mountains, and an hour later they were climbing them. They made their way along the sides of valleys, the road like a gutter hacked across the steepness. There was snow everywhere and vast knobbed icicles hung from cliffs and from the glacial sluices in the crevasses between the valleys.

Beneath the rising road was a loud, almost demented-sounding river battering greeny boulders and crashing along the deep stone trough, uselessly shoving at the walls. The mountains had no peaks: they penetrated a ceiling of cloud that was like sky stuffing and that in places had slipped sideways to reveal in torn holes sky the color of tropical water — aquamarine that seemed as pure and soft as a harmless gas. She thought that oxygen must look like that. The snow by the roadside was pushed into precipitous heaps, and nearer Bourg-St.-Maurice what people she saw were either skiers or peasants — wearing absurdly bright colors and ridiculous hats, or else dark heavy coats and black boots.

The last ten miles to the high slopes of Les Arcs were a twisting ascent in which Lauren began to imagine herself upraised on a skyhook that made everything around her vanish — the cliffs, the ice, the pines, even the road — everything but the car in which she sat. The car seemed to tremble on an air current. Her ears crackled like static. She was in empty space and only she was real; but no — it was the whiteness of the snow.

The next day was sunny and bright, and she was amazed that at this altitude, among all this snow, she was comfortable and not even cold. She left her ski suit unzipped. She was in a beginners' class, on rented skis, very short ones; the resort was famous for this method.

"Are you alone?" It was an American woman sitting beside her in the chair lift. Lauren had taken her for a

German — she had German eyes: ice blue, humorless, lovely.

Lauren said, "At the moment."

"I was just wondering if you had a partner — a husband or a friend."

"I have both," Lauren said. "Periodically."

"I like you!" the woman said. "My husband's a great skier, but he's so competitive! He's at the Aiguille Rouge today. What's that — ten thousand feet? He wants to get dropped out of a helicopter somewhere around Mon-Blong. I got sick of staying in Vence, that's where we live, he's with GE. But I hate being a beginner. I was watching you stumble up to this lift and I thought: She's just as bad as me. I'm Ellen."

She had said too much; she had spoiled it, so all Lauren said was, "How big is the class?"

"Just the five of us from last week, and you, and that new guy." Ellen was pointing her ski poles at the man in the swinging chair in front of them — his head made smooth and compact by a snugly fitting ski hat.

"Here we are," Lauren said, seeing the man glide away from his chair at the top of the lift.

"Don't knock me over," Ellen said, and just as they arrived she panicked, shoved Lauren sideways and then tripped her.

Lauren was emptying the snow from the inside of her gloves when Ellen hobbled over to her. But, instead of apologizing she said, "Those chair lifts are hell!"

Lauren said, "I know how to fall."

But Ellen was looking at the new student. "I'm probably prejudiced but I have to laugh when I see blacks on skis.

He's probably a Hindu or something. Doesn't he look a little out of place?"

Lauren said, "I've seen them in all sorts of places," and there was an edge in her voice that did not invite reply from the woman.

Stumbling and slipping, falling in ways that looked comic but that were painful and embarrassing, the class — growing more frightened and less determined as it fell — zigzagged to the foot of the long slope. The instructor, a woman with red peeling cheeks and a faded blue ski jacket, stamped her skis and muttered in French, "*non, non, non,*" contemptuously as one by one each person in the class fell, negotiating a little half-hidden hump of snow.

Later in the morning, Lauren found herself next to the newcomer in the chair lift. She had wanted that, but had he helped? He was very calm, hardly looking at her.

"I'm studying the Arab world," she said. "Where are you from?"

He said, "The Arab world," and smiled. "But my business takes me all over. My parent company is based in London."

Why was it that only Arabs and Indians used expressions like "parent company"?

She said, "We must have an awful lot in common."

"Then we should have lunch."

"I'm just going to have an apple in my room."

He said nothing. They were arriving at the top of the lift. They struggled off without falling and shuffled to where the class was waiting.

"Do you have two apples?" he said.

At noon, he knocked on her door carrying a large basket of fruit wrapped in cellophane and ribbon. He had a yard of French bread and a small wheel of Camembert and two bottles of wine. Typical Arab overkill: he could have brought one apple. But she was getting to like the needless gesture and found it a comfort.

She said, "I don't drink, but I sure do like bananas," and removed one from the basket and peeled in a slow un-zipping way, with her teeth.

They sat by the window and stared at the luminous blue snow and the white sky and the spindly black pines. Now it looked very cold outside.

Lauren said, "I should tell you, I'm alone at the moment, but I'm waiting for someone."

The man nodded; had he seen something outside?

"My father," she said.

"We'd better hurry," he said, and touched her, though he was still peering outside.

"We've got plenty of time." She began wriggling out of her ski suit. "I hate wearing all these clothes."

They missed the afternoon class, and when they awoke from the short deep sleep — was it the sex or the altitude? — it was snowing. The flakes were large and loose, as big as fur balls, and swaying past the yellow lamps that lined the buried path beside the hotel.

His name was Sonny, but probably not, and he might have been from Syria — he was very vague and he also mumbled when he seemed unwilling to reply. She did not want to know more: there was always a commitment in asking questions and expecting replies, and she knew she often became unreasonably eager when she heard things like "I'm looking for someone to run my Qatar operation."

He was handsome — watchful, appreciative, very strong. He made love to her in an old-fashioned impaling way — it had been months since a man had done that, and he surprised her by chafing her into orgasm. Then it was like levitation, a midair feeling, and all her nerves singing — energy in her fingers and toes — until the orgasm shook and scorched her and she fell back to earth and began to cry. She tasted her tears; she was proud of them; she gave herself to them and faked them a little more until Sonny was pleased and frightened.

"This has never happened to me before," she said.

"Some women never have one."

"I mean, the crying," and she let the tears dry on her cheeks.

After that they skipped most of the classes. She used the sauna and the exercise cycle in the hotel's health club, and Sonny fed francs into the electronic games in the resort's game room. Lauren liked watching him play the idiotic video games, seeing him amaze the young French boys with the rattle of his enormous scores. "They call this 'Frogger' in England, but here it is called 'Jumper.'" He played that croaking one reluctantly. He preferred the high-speed rocket chases and machine-gun games that were full of asteroids and explosives.

It seemed a just revenge on the skiers, who were either experts or incompetents. People came for one week to learn how to ski! Then they came the next year for an-

other week! It was exhausting, dangerous, expensive and
— Lauren thought — pure showoff. Did anyone ever ski
alone? The idea was to have someone watching you do
it better than they could. Something in the whole ski
thing reminded Lauren of details she had heard about
health spas a hundred years ago — immersion cures and
colonic irrigation and "taking the waters" and generally
going to a lot of trouble in order to justify eating well and
meeting people and getting laid at a high altitude.

The first two days she forgot about everything except
meeting Sonny and making love. This was the kind of sex
she had been denied in London. She needed him for it; she
loved it, she ached. It was certainly better for you than
skiing. It was always in her room, and he always gave her
time to herself. He had a lot of sense for an Arab: he
cared about her pleasure.

"What about your father?" he said on the morning of
the third day.

"My father —" She looked pained: agony. Her father
was dead.

Then she remembered.

"I'd better call him."

It took her the whole morning to get a line, and when
she reached the Holiday Inn in Geneva the line was bad.
"Speak louder," the operator said, but Lauren was already
shouting. She screamed her name, she spelled Lord Bulbeck's, and then hung up, hoping the operator was deaf-
ened by the crash of the receiver — but they never heard
more than a click, did they?

The phone call worked. That evening there was a tele-

gram: REGRET UNABLE TO MEET YOU. WILL RING YOU ON
RETURN TO LONDON. No signature — what a cautious man!
— but she knew who it was from.

Sonny was playing Moon Landing in the game room,
working a jolting vehicle and firing with it at looming
monsters. A crowd of French children had gathered
around him and looked very impressed.

"He's not coming." She didn't say "my father" — it
gave her the creeps to say the word now.

Sonny said, "I've earned five credits. That's a free
game."

"You know where I'll be, darling." She went to the
hotel to exercise and change. She liked this life here: she
wanted more of it — not the skiing, but everything else.

She waited until ten o'clock. Her certainty and her
anticipated pleasure made her patient. But just after ten
she craved an orange and called Sonny's room to remind
him to bring some. The phone was dead. She dressed and
went looking for him. His room was locked. He was not
in the game room. On a whim she asked at the front desk.

"He checked out two hours ago. He is gone."

Why did the French seem to take such pleasure in
giving a person bad news?

She went back to London and at last, after an
unexplained two weeks without seeing her,
Lord Bulbeck phoned her at Half Moon Street and said
he wanted to take her to a play. It was a West End revival
of *A Streetcar Named Desire*, but she insisted on leaving
at the intermission.

She said, "Tennessee Williams would hate my guts. But it's a phony play, so that doesn't matter. Only a fairy could have written that play and gotten everything wrong."

Lord Bulbeck said, "I can't imagine anyone hating you."

"I'm the sort of healthy open-minded girl that people used to call a nymphomaniac," she said.

They went to the Savoy Restaurant. Lord Bulbeck asked to be seated in a corner, away from the view of the Thames. Lauren had two appetizers and nothing else. Lord Bulbeck had smoked buckling, and then steak and grouse pie, and finally sherry trifle.

"You're killing yourself," Lauren said.

Lord Bulbeck wiped his mouth and ordered a schooner of port. He said, "I missed your dire warnings. And I missed other things."

"I thought you'd forgotten about me. You never came skiing. It was fun."

"I had to return suddenly to London."

"You still haven't visited me here!"

Lord Bulbeck said, "But you moved to a new place."

"That's just it. I wanted you to see it."

He said, "I wonder if it's safe."

"Everyone worries about me!" Lauren said. "I can take care of myself!"

"I meant me," Lord Bulbeck said. "I have to be very careful you see."

He was eating the sherry trifle still. His conversation was always full of maddening pauses when he was eating.

"It's my views." He chewed and swallowed. "I'm on a certain council — I'm chairman. Improbable as it may seem," and he chewed and swallowed again, "some people have threatened me with trouble."

As always she was fascinated and distracted by his pronunciation. He said "sherry tryfoo" and "cownsoo" and "improbaboo" and "peepoo" and "truboo." But what was he talking about? She wondered whether it was an upper-class accent, and she suspected that it wasn't. But it was lovely in its way. Why was the poor man looking so serious?

"— getting used to peroo," he was saying.

Could that be *peril?*

Now he changed the subject, perhaps because she had been so interested in his accent that she had not said a word. He said, "I suppose you've been seeing other men?"

"Seeing them, yes."

"I imagine they just want to get you into bed."

"*Bed?*" she said. "Bed? I haven't been in bed with any-one for weeks. You're the only man I go to bed with."

Lord Bulbeck said, "You're joking, of course."

"I'm serious," she said. "On a table, on a chair, on an exercise bike, in the bathroom — yes. But not in a bed."

"How is it to make love on an exercise bike?"

Lauren said, "He was taking pictures of my thing."

"And a bathroom," Lord Bulbeck said, making a face. He was hardly listening. Sex was so often a completely private set of fantasies.

"We weren't making love," Lauren said. "He was shaving me."

Lord Bulbeck said, "But not shagging you."

"No. But last week I came close. I've got this other guy who takes me out. He's an American engineer, working on weather satellite technology. He's got this girlfriend, Debbie. She's from Scotland and she's got this really neat accent. Usually we go to his place and he puts on a video. It's always something dykey. Then we watch it and he gets Debbie and me to start kissing. I mean, we really make out. Is that what shagging is?"

Lord Bulbeck had become very intent. He swallowed, concentrating hard, and said, "Then what happens?"

"Then he fucks Debbie while I watch and then we all go out to dinner," Lauren said. "But I never eat anything except salad. I'm a salad person."

"Go on about the other thing," Lord Bulbeck said.

What *other thing?* she thought. She said, "Well, you mentioned bed, but there isn't much of that. Men don't want a woman. They want an object. I mean literally. 'Stand very still,' they say. They want me to be a pillow or a chair or a table or a pet rabbit. They want me to be a *thing*. It's ridiculous!"

Lord Bulbeck said, "I'd like to go to your flat with you right now and take you to bed."

"Yes, yes," she said. "That'll be a change."

"I'm quite in the mood," he said. He paid the bill and they left the restaurant.

She said, "It's good for you to leave the rest of that dessert. And coffee is just horrible."

They went to Half Moon Street. Lord Bulbeck went into each room, sniffing, touching, looking out of the windows. "There's the famous exercise bike," he said. He reminded her of a detective searching for clues, and when he was satisfied that there were none he undressed with his usual care, one cuff button then the other, and shaking each leg out of his trousers, and piling everything onto a chair. It was the clear plastic chair. She had not told him about that — how she pressed herself against it for Karim.

She wanted to say "Sex isn't sex — at least, that isn't." It was rarefied and distant and private, the small corners of private fantasies. Now she and Lord Bulbeck were in her bed at Half Moon Street for the first time, and he was stroking her slowly: like a lover, she thought. That was it — the men were not lovers. Most of them did not even touch her. She found it impossible to enter the feelings of these men. She tried: she wanted to share that thrill and to know that satisfaction. But there was only the ritual, the solitary orgasm, and no satisfaction. They probably didn't have any feelings at all. Sonny the great lover had just ditched her!

"Did I hurt you?" she said.

"A littoo," Lord Bulbeck said. "Why?"

"You moved!"

But she was joking, because he lay beside her, exhausted, looking mugged.

Later, she said, "I'm really glad you finally came here. This flat is special." She felt his hand on her: he had tried hard to please her. She said, "And you're special." But she could not use the word "lover" for someone with so many secrets.

8

When Karim said, "There is someone I want you to meet," she was prepared for anything. It was a silent man with a suitcase. The suitcase made her reflective. The ones who used props always seemed a little unsteady emotionally — even Karim and his camera, the way he poked the thing at her. And as with some of the others Karim insisted that she take this man to Half Moon Street.

That day, Lauren had agreed to read a paper at the Thursday seminar which covered topics of current interest — General Newhouse called the papers "backgrounders." Lauren did not have a paper, nor had she submitted any work to the Fellowship Committee. She gathered newspaper clippings and wire service reports, and she filed and cross-referenced them with the financial analyses — anything to do with oil revenue investments. But all revenue was oil revenue! She wished she had never begun the project — China would have been easier, food would have been more fun; but she would still have had to face those scraps of paper and those fat files. She could gather material but she could not write.

Writing was so hard. It was not just setting down your thoughts or putting those clippings into a narrative, but more like learning how to think and then teaching yourself to write. It was not just hard — it was impossible for her. Her hand stiffened on her keyboard after the first *bop-bop-bop*.

She thought: I should get one of these word processors.

The Institute had a computer, with a telescreen and a printer. She sat at it with a stack of notes. *Chk-chk*. And then, *chk-chk-chk*. But it didn't think. It was a glorified typewriter. There was a game they played every Fourth of July on the courthouse lawn in Turkey Hollow — the peanut race. You pushed a peanut with your nose, six feet to the Civil War Memorial. That's what writing was; and she looked at her notes: this is my peanut.

And the task was much larger and sometimes when she was trying to write it was as if she were trying to invent the written word — like originating language itself. Impossible. And what about spending every night with those men? She was strong but she did not have time enough to write and also live her other life.

She did not write a seminar paper, but instead spoke from her notes. Suspecting that the others would think she was frivolous if she wore a dress — it was almost April but very sunny, and warm enough for her Laura Ashley pinafore — she decided on her tweed jacket and severe blouse and gray flat-heeled shoes. It was her usual escort outfit, her librarian look. "I'm naked underneath," she said, if a man questioned the style.

The title of her talk was "Work in Progress" — she wanted something loose and ambiguous. She had organized her notes around various headings — investments in energy schemes; buying foreign currency; recycling petrodollars; and spending on leisure. Because she was talking to historians and political scientists she decided to include some basic accounting terms and she began by describing the implied differences between expenses and expenditure, and other misunderstood financial terms. Then she turned to her headings and illustrated each one with a particular person — "I think the most effective methodology is the case study" — and she made her points by describing various men she had met through the Jasmine Agency: where their money came from, and where it went. She did not mention the agency. How shocked those men would have been! She said, "In an interview, the subject disclosed —

"Salim is fifty years old, from Qatar, and has a number of business interests, mainly in oil-related industries. On a recent trip to London he met with an American manufacturer of solar panels and placed orders totaling a half-million dollars. These were transshipped not to Qatar but to Pakistan, where Salim is developing an agricultural scheme. When interviewed, the subject disclosed —"

When interviewed the subject had been just behind her, furiously bumming her against a mirror. And similar impressions came to her when she discussed "Mamoun," her foreign currency case study; and "Hamid" the film importer; and "Ahmed" and "Jabari" and "Fadhel" — the last three were all friends of Karim whom she entertained at Half Moon Street, and whom she suspected of being arms dealers. But she used them to illustrate property and leisure.

General Newhouse, as chairman, summed up her talk by saying, "This can hardly be called rigorous analysis, but a study of this kind has great charm and subtlety as well as insights. There is considerable merit in this. Questions, please."

Lauren loved answering questions, and she easily turned them to her advantage: "And this reminds me of something else I meant to emphasize —" Her talk was not well documented — it was not documented at all. But she knew that it was appreciated for being fully human. She had made events and abstractions understandable by describing the men behind them. The men had paid her for her companionship or her sexual performance — but so what? It really was scholarship, of a kind, and later when she was praised she thought: I've earned that.

It was on the afternoon of her successful talk that she received what had become a daily call from Madame Cybele. Somehow, she expected her to say "Bulbeck." She said, "Karim." And Karim said, "There is someone I want you to meet."

He did not at first show her his suitcase. He met Lauren at a prearranged spot — the gazebo in the center of Berkeley Square: she watched the daffodils tremble as she waited — and it was as they were walking together back to Half Moon Street that he pro-

duced the metal valise. One minute there was nothing, and
the next minute this heavy thing was bumping his leg —
certainly heavy, because his arm was straight and tugging
his shoulder at a slant. He said his name was Zayid —
volunteered it, and so she knew he was lying. People
seldom lied to her: what was the point of lying to a
stranger? A stranger was one of the few people in the
world who could be trusted with the truth.

Lauren's successful talk that morning had made her
confident and bossy. She took charge and became in-
quisitive — Where was he from? What did he do? How
long was he staying in London? He said nothing, which
unsettled her — silence always did — and then when she
persisted, for her own peace of mind, he said, "I am
engaged in various sorts of business," and no more.

His English was good: he could have explained. But he
stayed strangely silent — so different from the boasting
men she was used to.

Zayid grinned at the room, at the street, at the pavement
below, at the rooftops. It was a grin of wonder — his
smiling lips and bared teeth expressing incomprehension.
Lauren had seen this grin on the faces of nervous men in
hotel rooms when they faced her. But Zayid was facing
the windows.

"Will you have a drink?"

"That will not be necessary at the present moment."

He had the foreigner's pointlessly good English — too
many words. In this way he reminded her of Madame
Cybele.

He did not "require" any food, he did not "use" cigarettes, he had a "very sweet tooth" and where was the

"parlor"? Talking this way he seemed to be turning aside — Lauren always found formal English suspiciously evasive. And she could not understand anyone until the person acted. Because this man was not saying or doing anything she did not know him. She had weeks ago stopped looking for motives in men's faces. She could handle men. After she made them come they were silly and embarrassed. It was one-sided sex — she got nothing — but she sometimes maliciously thought of it as castration. Men were so empty afterward!

When Zayid took out his camera Lauren relaxed — the voyeurs were always the silent, reticent ones, just spying on a body, hiding near it and possessing it at a distance, like certain travelers. The voyeurs were harmless. Taking pictures was not sex — that act was a private moment, later, when the pictures were developed: hot hands and bulging eyes.

But Zayid's back was turned. He was pointing his camera out of the window.

Lauren said, "The Naval and Military Club. They don't let women in. Isn't it awful?"

He did not face her. Had he heard?

She said, "But then, you probably approve of that."

Nothing.

She wanted to call Karim and say, "Hey, where did you dig up this guy?"

He was a small cold man. His grin, which looked like understanding, was incomprehension; his frown, which appeared to be concern, was complete indifference. I can understand sex, and I can understand the fetishism that turns things into sex, she thought; but I can't figure in-difference.

She said, "I've got to make a phone call."

"No phone calls."

"Don't say 'No phone calls' like that! You're not my father. I want to call Karim."

"Karim is no longer present in this country," Zayid said.

"What's that supposed to mean?"

Zayid frowned: he didn't care. "Ring him if you like."

She tried — anxiously aware that she was breaking agency rules — but there was no answer.

"He's probably out."

"He is definitely out."

It worried her that he seemed to know so much and that he did nothing. He had put his camera away and had stopped pacing the room. He sat down in a chair by the window and went to sleep: was he going to spend the night there?

Lauren did not want to go to bed while he was in the chair. She started doing her stretching exercises, then be-came self-conscious and stopped. She lay opposite Zayid on the sofa with a pillow under her head, but her inter-rupted routine — the presence of this man — kept her awake. She did not mind missing dinner, but missing exer-cise made her restless.

"Where are you going?" Zayid said, without moving in the chair.

"Out. I can't sleep. I'm going to run."

"Stay where you are," he said. "You forget I have paid you."

Six hundred pounds in a brown envelope — such a thick packet she had had trouble crushing it into one of her shoes in her closet. But she had forgotten the money, because she hadn't done anything to earn it.

She said, "What do you want me to do?"

"Exactly what I say."

That worried her and her worry increased when he remained silent for the next three and a half hours, his lids not completely down and his nighthawk eyes shining through crescent slits.

Just before dawn, he said, "We go."

She was ready: she had not taken off her track suit.

They walked to Berkeley Square down wet yellow-black Curzon Street, passing a policeman and then two gamblers — who else would be here at this hour? And she was reminded that Zayid had a gambler's wordlessness. At the top end of the square Zayid stopped next to a BMW and told her to get in.

"I'm always trying to get into the wrong side of the car," she said, crossing to the passenger side. "In the States the steering wheel's on the left."

He said nothing, but his driving put her on her guard: he drove one-handed, too fast, always flooring when the light changed, and turning sharply, trusting to luck that there would be no one crossing the road.

She said, "I hate these butch cars," hoping that talk might slow him down.

He sped south, past the Palace and across Westminster Bridge. She watched the signs and looked for something familiar.

"I know someone who lives here," she said, seeing a sign to Brixton. She was speaking of herself, in that room, in that house, hating London. She could not connect that girl with this woman, the past with the present.

"She's amazing," Lauren said. "She makes popcorn and feeds it to the birds. She's real strict about her diet. Like she eats carob? And bean curd? And about a ton of bran a day? She used to be married but she left the guy, because they were always arguing about curtains and whose turn to cook. She started off writing this book about Kissinger, and that got her interested in China. But she's been everywhere. She's always saying that the Chinese have beautiful skin, and Hindus never wear wigs, and Africans have perfect ears and — get this — Arabs never wear secondhand clothes. Jesus, do you have to drive this fast?"

He neither responded nor slowed down.

She said, "This isn't your car."

He glanced at her.

She said, "You weren't driving a car last night when you met me."

"How do you know that?" he said, surprising her with a full sentence.

"Because if you had come in a car I would have seen it and remembered the license number. I always do that, just to be on the safe side."

"What is the number of this car?"

She told him the three letters and the three numbers that she had seen when she had crossed behind the car to the passenger side.

"I knew last night that you were very clever," he said, and drove faster.

"Clever doesn't mean smart in the States," she said. "It means something else."

He said, "I mean something else."

"Where the hell are we going?" she suddenly demanded.

His fast driving was like a reply. They made their way through Surrey, and dawn struck at them — long fragments of light from the end of a long brown set of meadows. She stared at the rising sun until it became a bonfire on those meadows, and it gave the packed clouds in the high sky the texture of smoke. This was old orderly England, looking senile but safe; she preferred this to the trampled edges of London.

"Where are we going?" she asked. She was sorry her voice had a slight tremor of suspicion and fear in it. Perhaps that was the reason he did not bother to reply.

There was no conversation, so she read road signs.

"Godstone," she said. "Piltdown."

But saying these names into the silence made her uneasy.

"Listen, where are we going?"

He frowned and it meant everything.

Did he know where he was going? Perhaps he was just following any old road in order to speed. She had felt so differently yesterday. *There's someone I want you to meet.* And she had gladly agreed, because her seminar talk was out of the way — little accomplishments like that relaxed her and made her lazy again.

She felt she should deliberately try to make herself feel hopeful.

"I think it's so important to know when to relax. Some people don't know how."

There were wide hills in the distance with long smooth summits and shadowy hollows, and nothing behind them but great tumbling fumelike clouds.

She said, "Do you know where you are?"

He snatched at the gearshift and said nothing.

She said, "I want to go back."

He ignored her. He looked up each side road that they passed — fifty feet off the main road they narrowed to country lanes.

She said, "I have to go back. I've got things to do to-day —"

She had taped her seminar talk. If she got someone to transcribe it and she did a little work on it, she might be able to publish it. She wanted to get that going today, have a good night's sleep to make up for last night.

Zayid turned his face to her, but his eyes were not on her. He was looking past her at a narrow side road, and then he swerved suddenly and aimed the car into it, skidding as he went. Now they were racing down a country lane that was wet black from a recent shower.

She said, "Unsafe things always look lovely to me, like certain bridges and certain roads, and ice on a lake in the winter."

She was terrified and could hardly breathe.

"Would you mind slowing down?" Talking helped her get air. She only asked questions when she was afraid.

"Jevington," she said, as they passed a low black and white village sign. "Please stop."

But he swerved again on a yet narrower lane, hardly more than a path, that carried them steeply up a hill into some trees; the curves surprised him, but he did not let up.

She was sure that he had no idea where he was going. He was turning on impulse, looking for the narrowest road, the most hidden place, because — why had she gone when he grunted, "We go"? — he wanted to harm her. She felt freezing waves of a kind of murderousness coming at her from his body like a strong smell. She thought: He wants to kill me.

He was looking for a place, hurrying toward the end of this empty lane.

She said with useless anger, "What do you want?"

He stopped the car so quickly she felt a sense of forward movement for a few seconds after he stopped — it was a stomach-sickening weightlessness that was also fear.

He faced her and fumbled in his pocket — for a weapon, she was sure — but she already had the door open and was heaving herself out.

"Stay where you are!"

He said that last night when I wanted to run, she thought; and now she would run. She shouldered the door shut, wishing that she could tip the car over.

"Good morning," a gentle voice said. It was an old man, dressed for bad weather. He had a puffy friendly face and was carrying an umbrella and wearing a flapping raincoat. He stumped toward her in big muddy boots. Then he saw Zayid getting out of the other side of the car and grinning. The man blinked and said, "You're not local."

"No," Lauren said. He wouldn't touch her while this old man was near.

"I hope I haven't kept you waiting." The man took out a large black door key and said, "After you."

There, through an iron gate, and planted in the narrowness at the end of the pathlike lane, was a small country church with a low thick steeple — more of a plump tower than a steeple. The church was made of flint which, in the morning sun, looked like pieces of broken bone set into the sandstone walls.

Zayid was still grinning at the man. It was his wondering grin of concentration, all teeth and no pleasure. Then he grinned at the bone-white church. And then at Lauren. Whatever happens, you'll be sorry, his grin said.

The old man swung the heavy door open and said, "We don't usually get people this early. You must be keen."

"Tourism," Zayid said, as if replying to an immigration officer's question. He began talking, saying how pretty the church was. Lauren noticed that his English was much poorer when he was speaking to this old man than when he spoke to her. Everything about him worried her.

"Down from London?"

"No. We were in Brighton. Vacationing and seeing the sights."

He stared at her, daring her to challenge the lie.

"Eastbourne's much quieter," the old man said, and the church walls cushioned his words. "I often go down on a Sunday afternoon if the weather's fine. Planning to be in England long?"

Zayid said, "That is entirely up to my wife."

There was something about this obnoxious lie that made her certain that he intended to kill her. The word "wife" was like a rope around her neck.

"This church goes back to the tenth century," the old man was saying. He pointed with his umbrella. "That sculpture in the wall is even older — it was found in a stone chest under the floor of the belfry. It's Christ killing a demon."

A biscuit-colored chunk of stone sealed into the wall like a huge tile showed in relief a smooth almost feature-less Christ driving a spear into a beast's open mouth.

"That's Saxon. Fifth century, you could say."

Zayid grinned at this: his grin was fury and frustration. He walked down the center aisle, his footsteps ringing on the hard floor. The church smelled of cold paint and waxed wood and damp stone and dangerous roof beams. Ham-mer beams, the old man was calling them. The bare altar was set in a small enclosure, with an arched entrance.

"Chancel arch," the man said, hurrying after Zayid, who was grinning at the stained-glass windows. Lauren was backing away. "See those squints?"

He drew Zayid aside to the narrow openings.

"You'll never guess what they were for."

Zayid showed his teeth. It was his way of struggling.

"Lepers," the old man said. "But they were cut on the slant so that the lepers could see the altar from outside the church. You know what lepers are?"

Zayid's gaze lingered on the old man's tongue, as if the words were still there, and he turned his back on Lauren for the first time while he examined the squints in the arch, saying, "Leprosy?"

By then Lauren was pushing open the door to the porch and before the door swung shut again she was away, running hard down the lane and through a wet meadow, which was a long hillside at the edge of the Downs. From the top she saw the open sea and at the shoreline in a flat valley the town of Eastbourne — though she did not discover its name until she was well inside it and running toward the station.

The train arrived in London just before noon. In the taxi she resolved to pack and go, to leave London at once. Her fear had left her and now she felt a trembly euphoria that she was still alive — lucky!

Out of caution she alighted from the taxi at Stratton Street and walked slowly to Half Moon Street, making sure that no one was watching her. Then she hurried upstairs to her flat. She opened the door and stepping into the room she fought for breath — she steadied herself against the door jamb so as not to fall.

The flat was empty. It was not robbery — robbery was a sort of piecemeal plunder, the smash and clutter of things opened and broken. This was something else: it was clean and complete. Everything that had been there was gone — every stick of furniture, every carpet, every picture, every fragment of decoration. Her shoes, her money, her precious coat, all her books. It had been totally emptied, and she was frightened by the nakedness of the place. There was one object — the metal suitcase that Zayid had brought. It was pushed against the wall and in its small solitary way it looked dangerous. The other thing about empty rooms was their obvious stains — the faint trace marks where everything had been.

The bare flat — everything gone — gave the place an

absurd nightmare look and convinced her that someone had intended her to be part of this scheme, taken away like all the things she owned: someone wanted to kill her. She felt weak and terrified as if what she was seeing in these hideous empty rooms were symptoms of a fatal illness.

9

Now the flat seemed very dangerous — like a deep unmarked hole — and the cracked bricks on the buildings of Half Moon Street squinted at her in a threatening way as she passed them, hurrying toward Shepherd Market. She had nothing, she was naked under her track suit, she was cold without her mink-lined coat. She did not have her briefcase to take to the Institute — not even a pen! But what was the point of going to the Institute? She was finished here, she had been plundered: they had removed everything but her body. It was a fright that convinced her that she was helplessly close to death.

The Jasmine Agency was shut, though she went there anyway to make sure, not knowing whether to barge in and take a chance or to lurk outside. She lurked long enough to find out that it was closed. But it was usually closed in the daytime: the sleazy greedy places and the ugly girls were for the afternoon in this part of Mayfair.

It would have been a relief to find Madame Cybele. There was no one else Lauren knew who would offer help. She could not call up anyone and say, "Help me — I'm in trouble" — no one in that whole city knew her well enough: no one knew her at all or understood both of her lives. To those who knew her as a Fellow at the Institute she would have to explain how she came to be in this situation; so the Institute was out. And all those other men had paid her: there had never been any question of friendship. She had wanted it that way. Friendship was dangerous and cheap.

Karim had put her in this position. She hated him for sending Zayid to her. She wanted to call him and scream, "You failed — I'm still alive!"

But where was he? Zayid said he was not in the country. And what of Lord Bulbeck? The old secretive man now seemed as suspect and cruel as any other man she had known, and in her fear she began to hate him for everything he had hidden from her.

Men stared at her as she moved through Mayfair wondering what to do next. But only one move was possible: she had to leave. She had a little more than thirteen pounds in the shallow pocket of her track suit — the change from a purple twenty after buying her train ticket from Eastbourne.

Shepherd Market was full of travel agencies and ticket offices. She chose the agency with the most posters and asked the man at the desk the fare to the United States.

"Which city?"

"Washington," Lauren said. "No. New York."

"Is this first class or economy?"

Lauren pouted and said, "First class."

"When would you be traveling?"

"Immediately — today or tomorrow."

"That would be full fare, I'm afraid. Six hundred pounds, single. Just under, actually. Shall I book it for you?"

Thirteen pounds. Lauren said, "I'll be back."

Then she stepped into the street and a harsh voice behind her said, "I've been looking all over for you!" And at the same time a strong hand grabbed her roughly by the wrist.

She was naked on the floor of a darkened room and the man was standing above her and saying, "You don't sound as if you mean it."

"I *do* mean it," she said, in a pleading voice.

"No," he said. "You're lying. I don't believe you."

"Really," she said, and her voice broke. "It's true."

She pushed herself sideways to see his face. He was smiling. He wanted her to beg.

The man was short and had popping eyes and was bald under the nest of hair woven on his head. His penis was a blunt little thing, like a pathetic vegetable tucked under the hairy basket of his belly.

She said, "I'm dying to take you into my mouth."

"You're not going to get anything, my girl," he said, shielding the silly thing with his cupped hand. Then he was encouraged and he caressed it with his stubby fingers.

"Let me do that," Lauren said. "I'd love to do that. I want to touch you."

He said softly, "You can watch me."

"Yes," she said, and now she understood. They were always so evasive! "Let me watch you" — and moved nearer. "I love to watch you do that."

"Do you?" he said, and he repeated it. He was stalling. And he was stiffening — the vegetable had changed color and now filled his hand.

"That's nice," she said. But seeing him struggle she wanted to laugh. What a misshapen and ridiculous thing the penis was! Half of them didn't even work properly and all of them looked pathetic and detachable, like some wrinkled sea creature — like something you'd find goggling at you and swaying in an aquarium.

She had not touched this man. He had told her roughly to take her clothes off and to lie down on the floor ("Not on my bed!") and then he pulled the little demanding thing out of his pants and throttled it in his hand. Now he was whimpering as he dripped it on her and all its life was gone.

She said, "I love that," and propped herself up so that he could see her face. She was daring him to deny that she was telling the truth. "More," she said, and it was like mockery: he was done.

"Don't go," he said. "Please."

"If I stay it'll cost you another hundred" — she was already pulling on her track suit.

"Then go," he said. "You're a slut." He was at the door, fumbling with the locks. "You've got diseases. I wouldn't touch you for anything."

Lauren knew she had to leave quickly: men could be terrible just afterward in their humiliation. She had never

seen their famous sadness, but only guilt or anger or re-
sentment, or a sullen silence, as they realized they were
temporarily castrated — and how did they know at that
moment that it was not temporary? No man had ever completely satisfied her, or had touched her as tenderly and
deeply as she had touched herself. But she always knew
when a man's little frenzy was finished: they came with a
pathetic finality — one squirt and the rest dribbled and
that was all. This dope was still muttering as he shut the
door on her.

Following the signs to the fire exit she turned a corner
and saw a man entering a room.

She paused and stared and so surprised him he held the
door open. She said, "I bet your room has a terrific view."

"Dynamite," the man said, after a stutter of trying to
find the word. "Want to come in?"

"It'll cost you," she said, and stepped nearer and whispered. "I'll do anything you want. I just want to please
you." She implored him and stooped slightly and said in
a slavish way, "Anything."

The man showed a flicker of hunger and she knew she
had him.

By five-thirty she had turned nine tricks — the term
seemed hugely appropriate. Tricks were what most men
wanted. She had never solicited this way before; it excited
her and took the edge off her fears. The men were eager
— she guessed that they were able to smell other men on
her. And most of them, at last, were glad to see her go —
something to do with the daylight and the street noise and
their shame. It was so different from the night, when they
procrastinated and behaved like husbands, and whined

when she said she had to go. This afternoon showed her the laughable weakness of men — how they hurried, how impatient they were, how easily baited, how willing to pay. She stared, they faltered and fell. They were looking for her! She had almost twelve hundred pounds.

The good boutiques and chic stores were closed, but Selfridge's was open until eight that evening. She bought shoes, tights, a handbag, a Burberry and a lovely umbrella, and a silk dress. She left her track suit in the changing room. Returning to Park Lane she stopped an Arab dressed handsomely in a *thobe* and *besht* as he was entering the Grosvenor House Hotel.

"Yes, please, madam," he said.

But she had only smiled.

"Can you come with me?" he said.

He brought her to a third-floor suite and a man in a *dish dasha* opened the door and let Lauren in. He waved the other man away.

An Arab wrapped loosely in a towel lay sprawled on a bed, and the man in the *dish dasha* returned to him and in a loving way massaged him.

Lauren said, "I can do that."

The masseur glared at her, but the man being massaged said, "Come here."

She did so, towering over him. He took one of her buttocks in his hand and squeezed it and said, "I want this one."

"If you bum me," she said, "it's four hundred."

He said no, but in his eagerness to send the masseur away he miscounted and she got six hundred.

"Stay," he said afterward, but she said she was busy —

she did not have time for the drink, the dinner, the belly dancer and the groggy argument at midnight over where she would sleep. She felt enterprising and alive again: she had very little time left. Her goal had been a thousand pounds, but now — even after having bought those things — she had more than twelve hundred again and she decided on two thousand pounds even, like a gambler aiming for higher stakes in the middle of a winning streak. She would work all night — she had never stayed up all night before; she would leave in the morning with her money and her first-class ticket. Her tremendous panic was gone. She thought: I've got a hot hand.

She felt powerful — excited and greedy; she felt more willing now to take a risk, having survived what she was now sure had been an attempt on her life. She had nothing to lose; there was no one left to impress. She was indestructible. All she had to do was stay away from Half Moon Street.

She stopped men on Piccadilly. They wanted to be stopped by a pretty girl. She said, "I'll do anything you want. It'll cost you, but it'll be worth it." The mention of money made the men eager, for the only thing they had was money.

She sat at the bar of the Hilton and touched the man next to her and said, "Do you want me?"

He murmured.

She said, "Lead the way. I'm your wife."

After midnight the men were louder and rougher. She met them in doorways and they hurried her to their rooms. They had been drinking. The whiners of the afternoon were now asleep; these others were wilder and alcoholic and barely intelligible, but full of insistent and elaborate instructions. One man made her suck him off in the bathroom in front of the full-length mirror; another gave her a vibrator and explicit directions and he photographed her using it on herself; a third had her kneel over a chamberpot and piss while he drunkenly swayed before her and ejaculated against her cheek.

By the time the casinos were closed — three-thirty or four — she had been photographed again — but with her face turned away. She was bruised and had scratches on her arms, and she was saddle-sore from the bummings and the pokings. And yet no man had lain between her legs and simply fucked her as Lord Bulbeck had done last week: they were too frightened, too shy, and they were indifferent to her pleasure. Did they know how identical they were in their fears?

She had lost track of the men, of the foolish routines, of the numerous showers that still had not removed that hot oystery smell from her. But in the Ladies' Cloakroom in the Dorchester she counted her money. She had two thousand three hundred and forty-three pounds in cash. She thought: I'm free.

There were lights burning upstairs at the Jasmine Agency. She had seen them first in the early hours of the morning as she passed under the window with another nameless man, and she had thought fondly of Madame Cybele. Lauren's bruises inspired a sort of affection and pity for the woman.

But this ache made her feel slightly diseased, too, and there was something like an illness in the male smell that she could not wash away. The past hours had given her an understanding of Madame Cybele, and she wanted to see her to say goodbye.

She had to say goodbye, because she knew she would never go back; and what she had once regarded as enjoyable, the calculated frolic of a double life that had granted her a kind of power, she now saw as a sickening weakness, a feeble plotting to serve a bad habit.

She hated men now — hated them for being bullies and not caring about her pleasure. She hated their gross bodies. She hated their smoking and drinking — their decay. Most of all she hated them for not having any secrets. Their real malice lay in being both stupid and strong. They could have anything. They wanted the worst things. She thought fondly of Debbie, and how they had kissed and licked like two cats in front of the video while that man watched them.

The street was empty. She was walking in the direction of the agency. She felt sisterly toward the woman. She wanted to tell her that she understood and she was free. And she had a desire to warn her — to tell her to get away and escape while there was time, as she planned to do herself on this new day. Lauren was out of danger, but this realization made her want to save one other person. It was only fair.

The steep stairs reminded her of her first visit the day after she had seen the videotape — the stranger who knew her well and sent it had never admitted the fact; and then the two Arabs had said, "We want this one," and she had been flattered, and she had so easily stepped into this other life.

She took the stairs softly, one at a time, and heard low voices — one was Madame Cybele's, the other was a man's, perhaps Captain Twilley's. She knocked and there was a silence — the darkness of dead air. She listened at the door and knocked again.

She heard a drawer shoved into a desk.

"Come in."

Madame Cybele was alone, at the secretary's desk, looking up, trying to speak.

Lauren said, "Why do you look so surprised?"

Madame Cybele struggled to speak and then, unable to make any noise, she got up and rushed forward and hugged Lauren so tightly she was on the verge of tipping the tall girl over.

"Hey, what's up —"

"Who is it?" came a complaining voice from the other room — not Twilley.

Madame Cybele said, "Run!" and Lauren realized that the woman was trying to push her out the door. But Lauren was having trouble standing. Madame Cybele did not say anything more — did not have time — for in the next instant the speaker from the other room came to see for himself who the visitor was.

"Let go!" he shouted.

Lauren looked up, but she choked when she tried to speak — she was suffocated with fear. She stared at Hugo Van Arkady, who hissed at her in furious surprise.

10

He had taken charge, but he had not said much. He had paused only to gather his raincoat and his wide-brimmed hat and then he had hurried her to Park Lane and hailed a taxi. The streets gleamed — it always seemed to rain in London at this dark hour of the morning. He was giving the driver directions and she was helpless to resist. She was tired and shocked — they had made a fool of her. What affected her most was not the surprise that she had seen Van Arkady in that place, but the humiliation that he had seen her.

Now they were at Victoria in a first-class compartment, with the shades drawn, drinking tea out of plastic cups. The train was at the platform being loaded with mailbags and bundles of newspapers — every few moments there was a thump or a clang. Lauren faced the gaunt man. Ever since the taxi she had been asking him questions in a trapped and wounded way, but he had hardly spoken and he had not replied to her. Then, unexpectedly, he answered.

"You are catching the ferry to Calais."

"And you?"

"I'm making sure you catch it."

"I could have flown," she said. "I've got plenty of money."

"Money!" he said in a pitying way, as if it was the most meaningless thing on earth. He recovered from this word and said, "They'll be watching the airports. And you don't have much time."

"Why?"

He shook his head. "You'll be a great deal safer if you don't know."

"Where's my stuff?"

"Disposed of."

"Just like that," she said.

"Every bit of it is replaceable," he said with the same pity he had used to mock her with the word "money." "Your worry about it proves how young you are. It was such innocent junk."

She said angrily, "And you were going to dispose of me, too!"

"Zayid was supposed to take you away. His plane was leaving from Gatwick yesterday afternoon. That's why you ended up in that part of Sussex —"

So Van Arkady had been listening to her questions and pleadings in the taxi: her story of the car journey and the little flint church near Eastbourne.

"— He might not have killed you. It wasn't in his orders. But these people sometimes use their own initiative. It is cheaper to kill someone — and less trouble, and it's final. Don't say 'murder.' Simplicity can often seem very savage. This tea is disgusting."

"He was a savage."

Van Arkady considered this. "Because he didn't make love to you?"

"How do you know that?" But she had the answer as soon as she spoke. "You bugged my flat, you knew everything, you set me up."

He said, "You were our bug," and seeing Lauren wince, he added, "You were a live wire."

"You and Karim knew all those men."

"Not very well. We were listening to them, not you. We've never had a bug like you. Education is a wonderful thing."

"That's why you needed me," she said.

"Not really. You asked them good questions, but it was more a matter of security. You were one of the few people I trusted — you were completely reliable in your innocence. When I saw you at the General's party I realized you needed us."

She said, "You're the person who sent me that tape."

"I thought it might interest you. You seemed ambitious." Now he looked at her almost in admiration. "God, you were busy! You must be very healthy to keep up that pace. But you were also very lucky, you know."

"I used to think so."

"Yes. You might have been killed."

"By one of your slobs."

"By anyone. Listen, it's dangerous to sleep with every-one."

"You're a pimp and you say that to me."

Van Arkady said, "I hate that word."

There was a whistle, and the banging of doors, one after another, and shouts. Then there was silence and the train started, without any more sounds. The posters slid by, then a brick embankment, a bridge, a power station, rooftops and back yards looking derelict in the drizzly light.

Van Arkady smiled at the gloom. At lampposts a soft brown murk surrounded each saucer of light. He said, "London is an excellent place for murder."

She followed his gaze and then looked back at him. He was still smiling.

"It's quiet and peaceful, the police are unarmed, and if you're caught you get a fair trial. There is no torture, no hanging, no firing squad. The sentences are remarkably short and the prisons are clean. Do you know that the best-fed people in Britain are prisoners? Any murderer can study for a degree in sociology. Our people are used to a different sort of justice."

She said, "You do mean murder, don't you?"

"Never mind."

"It was something to do with the flat on Half Moon Street and my name on the lease. What is it, a hiding place?"

He said, "I hate intelligent people. You can't shut them off. Ignorant people can be nags but they're much more useful."

She said, "I know it's Half Moon Street."

"Your personal effects are gone. You should be glad they are, instead of sitting there pleading for them back. Zayid was just a courier, and you don't know anything."

"Why did you mention murder just then?" she said, and when he didn't reply she said, "You're an incredible phony. If those people at the party really knew you, they'd despise you. You're a pimp, you're a sneak, you run an escort agency in order to spy on the poor fuckers you don't trust."

He said, "I find you extremely ugly."

"And you're planning to kill someone."

He said, "You worked for us, darling."

"I could talk," she said.

"You won't. No one would believe you. And you'll never come to London again." He gestured out of the window at the last straggling suburbs, the semidetached houses, the allotments, the black canals. "If you come back, you'll probably be arrested."

"I don't have to go back to London to talk."

He did not hesitate. He said evenly, "You can still be killed."

She looked out of the window and saw a woman raising her arms to hang a blue shirt on a clothesline, and in the foreground a brickyard and BUILDERS' MERCHANTS behind a rusty fence; she knew at that instant that this was printed on her memory and that she would always see the woman and the brickyard and the sign and the fence when she remembered *You can still be killed.* Even in themselves they were horribly shabby, but they also signified his threat. These alone were reason enough for her never to come back and be reminded of what this man had said at the very margin of London.

In a small surrendering voice she said, "How long were you using me?"

"From the first," he said, and seemed triumphant. "Didn't you ever suspect?"

"Yes," she said. "Periodically."

He smiled broadly at her and she felt fooled in her lie.

"What if I hadn't moved to Half Moon Street?"

"We would have found someone else. London is full of people like you. The world is. That's why it is so easy for us."

"What do you mean 'us'? Who are you?"

He said, "The five thousand."

He did not speak again until they were near Dover. He fixed his eyes on her and his steady gaze seemed to emphasize the distance between them. She had no more questions.

"Don't look so sad," he said. "You're safe."

She thought: But I wanted to save someone else. She looked away from him, and now they were in a tunnel and her side window had become a mirror. Perhaps the other person I am saving is also me.

She did not relax when he was gone, nor when she was on the ferry, for she knew that though she could not see him he was still watching her in his own way. The surface of the Channel moved like a length of cloth in the turning wind. Lauren sat inside with a sad severe look on her face. At Calais the Paris train was enormously waiting at an empty platform. In Paris she bought a green leather suitcase and a cup of yogurt and stayed that night in an American-style hotel. She was exhausted but slept badly, because she was frightened, even here. And what was happening in London?

On the train to Roissy the next day she tried to put the past two days together. She puzzled with them but there was a large piece missing. And yet the rest was vast. There was too much. She thought: It hasn't happened to me yet. She was still trying to make sense of the first terrible day.

At the airport, all the papers on the newsstand, French and English — and every other language — had the same simple picture on the front page. It made a black pattern that ran through the display like a rack of wallpaper or linoleum. She bought *The Times*, *The Sun*, and the London Arabic paper, *Al-Arab* — in this one the picture was repeated larger than in any other paper, which was why she bought it. Here the fallen man not only had a face but an expression — surprise, anguish, and his eyes were whitened with fear. His hand was folded crookedly beneath him and great stains soaked his coat.

"Excuse me, miss."

One shoe was twisted away from his foot, and his narrow elderly ankle was showing. His frailty was obvious in his thin legs and in his brittle posture — he looked as though he had been thrown on those stairs, and broken.

"Are you — ?"

But it was this corpse's strange contorted posture that revealed his identity to her. His head and legs set so carelessly gave him an attitude that resembled ecstasy. She had seen him awkward and reckless like that a dozen times, and the last time exactly a week ago all twisted and looking murdered by his passion for her — and right there, too, on Half Moon Street. Horriboo, he would have said. She giggled a little and then began to sob.

"Are you actually reading that paper?"

She shook her head: No — and startled the stranger with her wet eyes and the way she pressed her lips into her mouth in grief. She made an animal motion with her hands — fear — and the man turned sharply away. Was he trying to pretend he hadn't said anything? But even as she watched him go she was still afraid and felt ugly.

DOCTOR
DE MARR

1

Out of nowhere, and after years of silence, George showed up one July day and put his face against the screen door and said, "Remember me?"

He was clowning in the way that desperate people sometimes do.

Gerald did not want to open the door. How could he have forgotten the man who had destroyed his life? He wanted to say: *I thought you were dead*. He had often hoped so, but his pessimism told him that it could not be true. George was his brother, or else he would not have let him in.

George was nervous, fussing with his hands and breathing hard, trying to be helpful. He followed Gerald into the kitchen and tripped him — almost knocked him over — he was so eager to please. Wherever Gerald turned he came up against his hovering brother. How different they were, and yet it had always been this way! Years ago, walking side by side, they had bumped shoulders, tramped on each other's toes, hit elbows — "You go first," "No, you." They got in the way, one kicking the other's feet, usually George kicking Gerald's, which was why Gerald resented the memory of being slowed and pushed by that little oaf. That was another thing: they were physically small — just over five feet in high school, and they did not grow any more. Gerald blamed his size on George, too. If it had not been for George he would have been a whole man.

Their father, who had no other children, used to introduce them at parties, saying, "I believe in having two of everything!" and he insisted they sing "Daisy, Daisy" while he sat there beaming at them. In those early years they wore the same outfit, had the same haircut and shirt. They wore shorts — knee socks and clunky shoes. Because of their size and their comic clothes they were always taken to be much younger than they were. Their father's intention was to make them look the same, but instead the identical clothes tended to exaggerate their differences. And yet people did not regard them as two boys but rather as one irregular being.

Gerald and George DeMarr were twins.

The hateful shriek was, "It's impossible to tell you apart!" It set them apart — it made them enemies. But, being twins, they could not be separated. They were a matched pair. From the first, Gerald and George were not allowed any existence away from this mirror image: each one was a reflection, or an instance of human repetition, or a small bodily stutter. They were seen as a double image. Gerald thought: I am a shadow, and it was an early mournful memory of his that as a twin he had been buried alive.

They seemed unusual, as physical echoes, and so they were goaded to perform. "Do something together — sing, dance, recite a poem, pledge allegiance to the flag." This was 1951. Their clothes were always costumes — just right for skits. They sang songs, they tap-danced until their bow ties shook loose, they did alternate stanzas of "Flanders Field" and "The Concord Hymn" (*By the rude bridge that arched the flood* . . .). It was all the hackneyed upbringing of being twins — the freakishness of it, the puppet show. People called them the Deedees, or the Dancing DeMarrs. It prevented them from maturing, it destroyed their will power, and this coupled with their small size meant they would always be treated as grotesques or as children.

"Are you sure *you* feel all right?" a person would say to one when the other was ill, as if it was impossible for them to escape each other's illnesses. They were not two individuals: they were aspects of one.

Their names, too, were given interchangeably, as if it hardly mattered. "You must be George," people said to Gerald, and they delighted in their mistake, because it was caused by the twins' sameness — and their flaw was that one was superfluous.

They grew up in a place that was both a town and a neighborhood of Boston — from the high ground in the center of it, looking east, they saw the Custom House tower, and to the west were wooded hills. The place itself was a barely respectable ruin of three-decker houses — dry, rust-colored shingles and sagging porches — on the very edge of the small city. Old Mr. DeMarr was a salesman in a men's clothing store that still called itself a haberdashery. It was a bad boring job, and unworthy of him, but his work had become an easy habit, and he was given discounts on his clothes. He dressed like a trial lawyer — pin stripes, a homburg, a cashmere topcoat. As a young man he had worn spats. He was slightly taller than his boys and very proud of his tiny feet. He told jokes; his wisecracks somehow fitted his natty clothes. The jokes revealed his sadness and his sentimentality. He was tearfully fond of his wife and always spoke to her in a shy grateful way — no wisecracks — because she never judged him and said what he feared, that he was a timid showoff and nearly a coward, who had pinned all his own failed hopes on his twin sons.

"Give them hell," he always said, when he goaded them to dance.

They were Catholics, and there was something about their version of Catholicism that took away their ambition and made them morally lazy: they had Heaven and the confessional and the consolations of secret rituals. There was a theatrical element in the Holy Mass, too, and it formed the twins and gave them a sense of timing and decorum. You had to perform to be a Catholic! They were altar boys, and then Boy Scouts, and later they tap-danced in the church hall: "for the glory of God." They were discouraged from joining any teams, since competitive sports would inevitably have emphasized their differences. A brief spell on the Saint Joe's softball team proved that — they couldn't both be pitchers, and George was the stronger hitter.

They were routinely given identical haircuts and identical clothes. For birthdays and at Christmas they were presented with identical gifts. Aunts and uncles were warned. If there were not two available of a particular thing, they went without — one was unthinkable unless, and this became common, a single gift was given: they were told to share it equally. That happened, as the years passed, with the rocking horse, the erector set, the pup tent, and the radio; each thing — *To Gerald and George, best wishes* — provoked a bitter and damaging quarrel.

For their first fifteen years or so they seemed to share a life as undifferentiated sides of the same person, one standing for the other, or else the shadow, or sometimes the ghost of the other — a sort of maddening mimicry that was vivid because their father had deliberately made them overlap. They lived a strange unseparated life, full of the hot secret dreams that are the sweats of frustration. They were in each other's company the whole time; they went to school together, they slept in the same room, they were never alone. It was symmetry of a kind, but it was ornamental, it went no deeper — all that effort purely for the design.

They hated each other from an early age; but they knew they had no one else. They were like the last two survivors of a race of people, with their own language and habits and customs. As twins raised in this way they constituted an entire culture, the smallest society on earth, a nation of two.

What enraged them most of all was that each believed himself to be totally different from the other. The very fact that they were twins made them obsessive about comparisons, and they never looked at each other without narrowing their eyes in scrutiny or, indeed, without discovering yet another crucial distinction. They glanced at each other as people usually glanced at mirrors, but they never saw reflections, only distortions.

Gerald looked at George and saw a shrimp, with small moles on his forearms that were more numerous in the summer; George looked at Gerald and saw a small pudgy coward. "You're pigeon-toed," George said. "You're worse — dink-toed." Gerald had a cowlick, George had a chipped front tooth. "You've got big lips," George said. "Not as big as yours." They recognized a vague similarity, but this made them monstrous-looking to each other. Each one seemed dark to the other and thought: I have a light complexion.

They knew that most people lived with the satisfaction that they were single and unique; but it was the fate of twins to be always weighed and compared. For the whole of their early life they were unhappily chained together, and it was torture to them, for the few likenesses they saw seemed like nothing more than ugly parody.

Their parents had connived at making them seem the same, but it hadn't worked; it never worked; the differences of twins were always greater than the similarities — yet only twins knew that. Gerald and George believed this. If they had been in the habit of confiding in each other they might have discovered that in this respect — in this one belief — they were identical.

When their mother died — they had just turned sixteen — their father held them tighter, consoling himself with them, treating them as toys, and goading them more fiercely. He demanded that they succeed, so that he would not be seen as a failure. And yet he was obscurely disturbed by the urgency of his demand because, as a failure, he did not know what he meant by success.

They were still at school. "George did ten laps," a gym teacher said once, challenging Gerald, who had been ready to give up after eight. He forced himself to do two more, and the next day he ached terribly from the effort.

"What do you mean you don't know how to do quadratic equations?" the math teacher said to George. "Gerald is a whiz at them!"

They supposed that George was being stubborn. He had to put in hours of extra study, and still he never got the hang of them.

This dreary competition inspired one day an unexpected response.

The Scoutmaster, Mr. Seagrave, said, "You don't know how to do semaphore?" He always shouted when he meant to be sarcastic, believing that sarcasm was not a choice of words but rather a certain degree of loudness. "But Gerald knows how!"

They were Senior Scouts and wore identical green uniforms and white leggings.

George put down the flags. In a flat insolent voice he said, "I'm Gerald."

Gerald looked up from his wood carving, and then smiled at his knife. How easily Mr. Seagrave had been fooled! It was a crucial victory, because it seemed to disprove what they had instinctively felt, about their differences being so obvious. They really weren't taken seriously at all, they weren't known, they didn't matter — no one looked closely enough to see them properly. It was the world's fault, either indifference or contempt. They thought: We are Chinese.

It proved that no one cared about them. There was no subtlety, no nuance. They were a pair — that was all. Their own father had not bothered to distinguish between them: "I believe in having two of everything."

It made them cynical. When they saw how easily they could be mistaken for one another they played upon the confusion. George took Gerald's driving test, and Gerald took George's French final. George appeared in court as Gerald on a charge of reckless driving — it seemed less serious that way. And Gerald worked as George at the Star Market. This last ploy worked so well they decided to share the job, putting in three evenings a week each bagging groceries and stacking shelves. This was in 1959, the year they graduated from high school.

All this had unexpected results. Their taking turns, and sometimes their monopolizing a particular subject, made their differences even greater. That last year of high school made them certain of this. Gerald, who had never really learned to drive well, seldom used the car. George was incapable of simple algebra, Gerald was ignorant of history, George of French, and Gerald would have failed art except for George's effort. Gerald had flat feet: the imprints on his foot examination were George's, but it was Gerald's good teeth that saved George from the dentist's drill.

Cynical people, who regarded them as freaks, had made them cynical and freakish: the two boys passed themselves

off as one nearly perfect specimen while remaining themselves — they knew — deficient in many ways.

George was the more composed of the two — a talker,
an easy conversationalist, full of plans and deceits. He attended all the college interviews and he made a good
impression, both as himself and as Gerald. Gerald had
become a silent and somewhat fearful person, and the more
George acted on his behalf the more his confidence ebbed.

But the college interviews marked the end of the odd
team effort, and soon the pretense was dropped and they
were returned to themselves. Their father died — that
dapper man who hid himself in his clothes; that puppeteer,
that sadist. Gerald and George were relieved and hopeful,
and they began to recover, as from a long illness. This
death had released them. The important witness was gone.
They realized now that their parents while living had in-
timidated them, made them guilty, and robbed them of
glory. Now the twins could quietly succeed or fail, and
now that they were free, each saw enormous changes in
the other. Using the insurance money they went to
college — different ones — Gerald chose Boston University and George chose Harvard. George flunked out in
his second year, was immediately drafted into the army
and was sent to Vietnam. He was not killed — Gerald
would have been informed of that as next-of-kin. It was
one of the sorrows of his life that he did not know what
had become of George; he brooded on his brother and he
felt sad and thwarted when he realized that he wanted
George dead.

Otherwise how could he live? He had earned his degree,

a B.A. in economics, and he worked in the Navy Yard as
a statistician. Sometimes he described himself as a veteran
and spoke about his adventures in various foreign posts.
He could even frighten some of the older men with these
stories: that snake, that lunatic, that fungus, that desolate
island. He did not say that he had never lived anywhere
except in the house his father had bequeathed him —
George had received a sum of money. Surely he was
dead? Twice, Gerald had almost gotten married — the
women were plain and seemed a little desperate and eager
to please; but it was they who left him. Gerald went on
living in the three-story house where he had been born
and raised. His lies were extravagant, but they satisfied
something in him and allowed him to live in a slow spare
way, almost monkishly. When he thought about George
he felt like a shadow and he blamed George for making
him feel insubstantial. Not that George had done anything in particular that displeased him, but rather that
George was alive. Whispers in Gerald's mind told him
maliciously that they were still being compared, and this
convinced him that he was living in a dumb and buried
way and that in certain respects he had already started to
decompose. Terrible thoughts — but he lived alone and
told lies and there was no one he knew who could dispute
his morbid thoughts.

Living alone, he frequently felt invisible, or only partly
visible — patchy and far off. It was a feeling of being half
there. Sometimes it was misery, and just as often it gave
him relief; but mostly it added satisfaction to the only
real pleasure of his shadow life, which was peering into
people's windows.

This spying thrilled him especially in the colder months, in the early darkness of winter afternoons, before curtains were drawn or shades pulled. He could look into lighted rooms and see people eating or standing at sinks. They stared, they fingered their buttons, they touched their faces. It made him short of breath to see these private acts taking place; and the sight of a woman in loose house-clothes, alone, combing her hair before a mirror, always held him and slowly throttled him. It gave him a taste for nighttime walks, and for trains; for back yards and certain streets. Until they pulled it down, the elevated train from Sullivan Square had allowed him wonderful window views. How he missed the curve where the train screeched and slowed between Thompson Square and North Station: several nearby windows in a gray house were his particular favorites, and he knew the furniture in them and most of the people. All windows tempted him, all rooms fascinated him from the outside, and the warm bright ones aroused him. Just the interiors, those secrets, had an obscure eroticism and always an excitement. But he knew it was pathetic.

And it gave him a hatred for the young. He did not know why. He had feared and despised youngsters his whole life, but now his hatred was corrosive. They were oversize louts who thought themselves to be unique. He envied them everything they wasted — they made him violently angry. They were older than they thought! Pot-bellied boys and blotchy girls — smoking had given them the lungs of fifty-year-olds. He enjoyed their ruin. They were most conspicuous in the summer months, squandering their health and shortening their lives on drugs. He

overheard things. "She's living with this incredible guy!"
he heard, or "He's absolutely devoted to his kids!" Such
remarks enraged him and made him murderous. But there
was justice in all things: they would get the early death
they deserved; but he who had never really been able to
choose — what twin ever did? — would go on living his
shadow life, for he had been shoveled under from birth.
And where was George?

Now Gerald was almost forty. Many people would
say he had had two lives, but he knew he had hardly had
one. Sometimes he remembered the skits and songs and
those performances — it was all mingled with religion, too,
the singing and ceremony with Catholicism and the mass:
God was the unblinking audience for whom every
Catholic had to perform his heart out. It was much worse
than an embarrassment. Gerald saw that its solemn foolery,
its clumsiness and its grotesque pathos made it actually
tragic. Tragedy was putting on the wrong clothes and
clowning and failing to be funny.

So the visit that July day amazed and frightened him.
The face against the screen. "Remember me?" The big
kicking feet. And one other thing.

"Deedee," the man said. He smiled at the secret name.

Except for that childish word, Gerald would not have
recognized him, and even so there seemed something
diabolical about the man in the doorway. The strong
summer light behind him had darkened his face and caused
his shadow to fall like a shroud over Gerald. The man
seemed calm in his darkness, but what unnerved Gerald
was the man's size: he was precisely Gerald's height.

Hateful little kids, some of them no more than twelve

or thirteen — girls of eleven! — were often his height. They roused his fury, yet he did not feel threatened by them. But now he had the experience of looking a middle-aged man squarely in the eye, and it terrified him to think that the man was his brother George.

"Where's your wife?"

Gerald hesitated, then took a breath to explain.

But the man said, "My marriage was a failure, too."

"I'm not a failure!" Gerald said loudly, but the way he said it revealed how frightened he was — it was a hollow protest.

"Don't be afraid," the man said — more calmly now. "I need a place to stay for a while."

Gerald said, "Why did you come back?"

"I never left."

Still, Gerald wondered: Is it George? George was the past, like an old coat and crippling clothes that Gerald had been forced to wear. He had nearly suffocated from the nearness of his hovering brother.

"Please go," Gerald said.

He opened the screen door but he stood his ground at the threshold, blocking the man's entrance.

"Are you alone?"

The man peered behind Gerald, and Gerald saw a stripe of light on the face — sunken features, dry lips, bright eyes. It was a glimpse of illness.

"Help me."

The man moved again, gave his face to the light. It was a small pale mask of hunger, and there was despair in the bony shapes.

"Please," he said.

Gerald stared back, wishing he would shut up and go.

They watched each other, broken-backed, in the same pleading way.

"Deedee."

That name again: Gerald gave in. He stepped away and motioned his brother in, and that was when George began bumping him and tramping on his feet.

"What do you want me to do?"

"Nothing," George said. "You don't have to do a thing. All I want is a quiet place to stay. I'm just paying a visit."

His tone was almost resentful, as if he wanted Gerald to thank him for asking such a small favor. That was typical. Because George wasn't asking more, Gerald was supposed to be grateful — grateful for granting him the favor. It was brother logic, and also the tyranny of twins. George's attitude had always been: *Be glad that's all I'm asking — my small request is a favor to you!*

"I don't want you in my life," Gerald said.

"We only have one life."

"That means two things," Gerald said. "And I mean one. This house is my life — I don't want you in it."

Gerald was afraid and spoke in a stilted speechy way, occasionally stammering.

"Look at me, Deedee." It was one of George's comic voices but it only increased Gerald's fear.

Gerald stammered on, weakening under his brother's gaze. "But I can't refuse to help you. I know you're desperate."

"I'm not desperate!"

George's panic had a calming effect on Gerald.

"If you're not desperate," Gerald said — slowly, as if teaching him English, so that he would remember the dig — "then why did you come home?"

As soon as he said it, he was sorry, because there was no possible reply. George just stood there and sagged a little in silence.

Gerald said, "The top floor's empty. I'll give you a week. But I don't want to be here with you. I'm going away —"

"Did you keep Dad's cottage at the Cape?"

"— and when I come back," Gerald went on, afraid of George's sudden interest in the property (he had an equal claim), "I don't want to see you here. Promise me that."

"I promise," George said, and when Gerald handed over the key George caught hold of his brother's hand lightly — just a squeeze, the same temperature, the same pads of flesh on the snagging fingers, and such a close fit that Gerald hurriedly shook his hand loose.

"Where's your car?"

"Bus," George said.

"One week," Gerald said, "starting tomorrow."

So it was final. George's back was to the window, and shadows had gathered on his face again — the small dark mask that had first frightened Gerald.

George said, "You look terribly worried."

"Never mind. That shouldn't concern you."

"It doesn't. I'm glad! When I see other people suffer I actually feel a whole lot better — sort of relieved that it isn't me! It sounds awful, doesn't it? But most people think that. Most people have devilish thoughts that they would never admit to. They don't even know that you have to be half full of evil in order to go on living. Do you still go to church?"

Gerald only watched, and what looked like worry on his face was anger — the hatred brimming in him at the sight of his brother mirroring his own empty life.

"I don't want to see you again."

"You won't," George said. "I know better than to ask a favor of you." It was his *Be grateful* tone. "I know when I'm not wanted."

But the top-floor key was in his hand, so he had it both ways, as usual. He had the favor and he also had the malicious satisfaction that Gerald had begrudged it. And just before he turned to go he did a soft-shoe shuffle and a little lisping flap of his feet. That was George: when he wasn't stepping on Gerald's toes he was dancing lightly in front of him — but each was a form of gloating.

George had gotten what he had come for. Gerald thought: But what about your sick face?

Gerald took his vacation then, two weeks early, and left the next day for the Cape. He sat inside the cottage most of the time, he fretted, mumbling to himself, always on the verge of crying and always blinking his glazed eyes: Buried again.

It was his first visit of the year. He had begun to neglect the cottage as he had neglected his life. The place was full of junk. He picked up his dump sticker at the Town Hall and took a miserable pleasure in using it, sitting there at the dump in his car, among the screeching seagulls, watching the bulldozer push the crates and bags into the pits of the quarry-like place. He liked the dump this week. He enjoyed seeing the filthy refuse covered, and there was something about this great noisy burial of things worn out and used up or pointlessly thrown away that he found consoling.

It rained most of the week, so it was either the dump or the movies. And the movies hadn't worked. It was one of those summer ones, for kids: a family on a farm, "If we all pitch in we can make it work," a sadistic neighbor, some dead kittens, the famous "drowning scene." When the struggling bag sank Gerald burst into tears and sobbed into his hands.

His hatred for George was making him ill. It did George no harm at all, he knew, but it was poisoning him. This hatred for his brother was like swallowing his own venom.

He gave it an extra day, to be perfectly sure, and then he drove home — embarrassed as he passed the gates of the town dump, where he had wasted those days.

There was no sign of George. But he had not come in a car the first time — perhaps he didn't have one?

I will take no notice of his absence. I will pretend it never happened. Yet he wanted to be sure, and so he was alert to every sound. As he unpacked his suitcase Gerald heard a mutter in the wall.

He ran to the back stairs and angrily used his own key. A radio was playing! So George hadn't kept his promise. Gerald noticed a faucet dripping as he crossed through the kitchen. *Now you've got to leave.* Gerald braced himself for an argument and trembled thinking, *You gave me your word!*

George was in an armchair. Obstinate: he did not look up. Gerald spoke his name. Very pale and plump — George was dozing. "Listen!" But George was obviously very sick. Gerald raised his hand to touch him, but the dry gray skin repelled him. So he whispered "Deedee" in a kindly way. But George did not respond, and then he knew that George must be dead.

Turning aside to whimper — it was a strange sound, like his soul leaving his mouth — he saw the hypodermic needle, the bottle, the ashtray, the addict's junk, and was that spilled soup in his lap?

2

Gerald had never known such a shock. Even the death of his parents and his guilty clinging grief had been nothing compared to this. This was physical in a paralyzing way, but it was slow and unstoppable, more like a fever: wave upon wave of emotion heaving within him and numbing him — sadness, surprise, relief, guilt, doubt, anger, joy. One caused another, washed up and broke, spilling useless surf and jarring his soul loose. It was hours before he could remember what had caused it, but even then he could not give this experience of contradictions a name. Afterward, he felt purer and slightly weak, as after a sickness.

For Gerald, George's death was more like an amputation — one that had been successfully carried out on his own body. It was as if a diseased and disfiguring part of himself had been cut away. It was a horror, and yet he could not think about it without feeling a little sentimental.

But it had been a necessary thing and, as with the death of his father, it had granted him another measure of freedom. There was a justice in its cruelty and, like all natural deaths in a family, it had an element of sacrifice.

George had brought it upon himself! The sick gloating man who had said how the sight of people suffering secretly pleased him — he had suffered and died. He had come home and killed himself, either accidentally or on purpose — pushed a needle into his arm and puked his guts out. His face still wore the urgent expression of the moments before death: defiance — he had fought back — and the only signs on his face that he had lost were his blue lips and cold eyes. His small cheeks were full, he was canted forward, plump and surprised.

And then Gerald wondered: Who is this man and why did he come here?

He feared that it might be merely a macabre joke being played on him; and what if it were not George, but just a small stiff corpse, propped on the chair to terrify him — not his brother at all? George was capable of a deception like that; it was the sort of thing George would enjoy. *You're next*, the staring eyes seemed to say. It was so easy to scare someone by surprising him, even if it was only to shout *Boo!*

Gerald began to loathe George for not being the dead man. Or perhaps it was the sort of convulsed and choking drug death George had endured that had changed his face and removed the resemblance — swollen his features and crooked his fingers. Or was it someone else entirely? This was awful! Before returning the third time — he could not think clearly in the same room as the corpse — Gerald had felt his anxiety giving way to relief. But with the new doubt as to its identity, he became anxious again. He had to be certain in order to be free.

The belongings in the man's pockets were too few to convince Gerald that it was George. It would have been so easy for George to have planted them. The dead man's face was bloodless and unrecognizable: pale unfamiliar flesh. Gerald caught himself pitying this stranger.

What if — Gerald was pacing the room downstairs, glancing at Boston through the front windows — what if it really had been George the other day, but that George had put this corpse here and dressed it in his clothes, given it his wallet and handkerchief: killed this man and thereby faked his own death? It was possible. And if that was the case he was depending on Gerald to report him dead, while he counted his money in Mexico or started a new life in California or wherever, and continued to cast his shadow over Gerald.

In the wallet there was some money — just over forty dollars — and standard wallet items, credit cards, social security card, all George's. There was no driver's license — that was odd; no photographs — even odder. The closet held an empty overnight case; some clothes on hangers, a pair of shoes. There was a razor and shampoo in the bathroom, and last week's *Globe*s, a sequence of three — Wednesday to Friday. Today was Monday. Did that mean the man had been dead for two days, or had things been arranged for it to look that way?

None of this matters, Gerald thought, if I don't know who it is.

But one thing did matter: secrecy. Gerald was certain

he would not go to the police. It might have been George, but if so, why should he dignify his druggy brother's memory with a decent burial? He had been messily buried by George for far too long. If it was not George then certainly George had planted it, and he would not do George the favor of reporting the death and aiding him in his pretense.

They were family reasons. There was a practical reason, too. The third story was empty because it was for rent — so was the second story, for that matter. There would be no possibility of a tenant if news of the death got into the papers.

Once, when they were children, the DeMarrs had been visited by their uncle Frank, who drove up in a green Cadillac. Frank was a simple soul and very proud of his car — practically new!

"Let's go for a spin," he suggested.

"You can drop us off at church," Mr. DeMarr said. He felt Frank was a dangerous driver, especially when Frank was trying to hold a conversation. But it was raining hard, and it wasn't far to Saint Joe's.

On the way, Frank said, "You won't believe this, but I only paid two hundred dollars for this beauty."

Mr. DeMarr sniffed and became thoughtful.

"Stop the car!" he said at last.

It was so loud, Frank pressed the brake and spilled Gerald and George onto the floor of the back seat. The four DeMarrs got out and walked the rest of the way to church in the rain, and it was not until they were inside that Mr. DeMarr spoke. He did so in a frightening way, hissing the sentence into his children's faces.

"Someone died in that car!"

And someone had died in Amato's duplex — years ago, and the place was still empty. "You'd hardly know someone died in there," Amato said. The *hardly* still bothered Gerald.

These recollections came to Gerald as he labored with the body, slipping it into a plastic bag and sealing it, and then dragging it into the garage and cramming it into a barrel. Upside down, and with the knees tucked up, it was just the right size. That brought back a memory: the pair of barrels they'd had in their act, and how they had been rolled onstage to the well-known song, and the twins had tumbled out and danced.

That memory continued, offering Gerald another glimpse of himself and George — George standing on his shoulders and wearing a long coat that reached to the floor, so that one on top of the other they made a whole man. It had been a life as little men, dedicated to dressing up and performing, and remembering it roused all his old hatred for George.

The next morning he awoke with a determination to get rid of the barrel. If it was George it was just what he deserved; and if it wasn't, why should Gerald worry? And there, lying in bed, still bitter about his hidden life, he hit on the perfect burial.

He was soon driving down the Southeast Expressway, keeping well under the speed limit. After Braintree the traffic thinned out. Gerald was penetrated with the vibrations of the wheels and he lapsed into a driver's reverie.

It was only as he bumped over the steel seams on the Sagamore Bridge that he remembered the load in the trunk; he began watching for the exit.

The dump lay behind a chain-link fence, and today the man in charge was examining dump stickers — making a business of it, halting each car and then, as it came to a stop, hurrying it, motioning with his hands in a peevish way and frowning, as if he found it all intellectually exhausting. Gerald was delighted to find the man there and not guarding the dump with his rake. Gerald was examined and waved on. He drove down the slope and parked near the narrow trench — it was just the width of the bulldozer that was filling it with the rubbish people heaved out of their cars in sacks and boxes. Among the dust and groans of the bulldozer were the seagulls — large nagging birds that mobbed the edges of the trench, occasionally tumbling in to tear at a burst bag.

Gerald waited for the other dumpers to drive away, and then he slid his barrel out and tipped it against the lip of the trench with the crates of grass clippings, and the lopped-off branches, and the smeared cans and broken beach chairs. He rolled it forward and it came to rest just beneath the bulldozed scoop, which covered it with half a ton of sand.

This must happen all the time, he thought. And he imagined the dump to be full of dead men and nameless errors and discarded mistakes, and all of it covered with yellow sand and household junk.

He remained — pretending to sweep out his car — until the trench was nearly full and the barrel completely buried. He trusted the incurious dump workers, but he had no such faith in the hungry seagulls. He drove away satisfied with what he had done. The corpse was small, but remembering its swollen features he thought: I'll never know.

I'm still on vacation," he said to the empty road ahead. He had the solitary person's habit of holding conversations with himself and always meeting opposition in these dialogues. "Call this a vacation!"

It seemed incredible that in such a short time he had managed to discover and hide a human corpse. He was a moderate, fastidious and decent man — he felt this strongly. Perhaps this accounted for his efficiency. He had always talked of his adventurous past, and talking had been enough. But now he had acted, he had taken a turning — for the first time in his life — and he had to keep going, to finish what he had started. The burial had made it complete.

He was alone, and so he was solitary in his deceit. It made him feel lonely, but not weak. In fact, he imagined that this secret gave him power, or at least an authority over his life that he had never known before.

He raced forward under hot gray clouds that had the shapes of sundaes and luffing sails. The horizon was a row of faces, with monkey cheeks.

As soon as he had crossed the canal he knew he had succeeded. The canal was like a break in time. He had left the past behind on the far bank: he was safe. There was nothing at all here to connect him with the corpse. It was perfect, a buried secret. But when he thought that the dead man might not be George, and that the whole business might have been a pointless risk, he grew sad. Perfection in such secrecy was sad enough, but it was all a paradox, because if it weren't a secret it could not be perfect. And anyway, who was there to tell?

He followed Route 3 toward Boston until, at Marshfield — feeling very tired — he pulled in to the rest area and parked. The sight of the river winding through the tall grass below the highway had always heartened him, because it was lovely and unspoiled, and his certainty that it was beautiful gave him hope: If I know that, then I'm still worth something.

He saw that he could leave the whole matter now and go home. No one would ever know. But another mystery would be his to ponder for the rest of his life.

He sorted the credit cards and rummaged in the wallet as he turned the matter over in his mind, wondering whether to pursue it. These cards proved nothing, and it was too late for fingerprints. That was when he found the laundry ticket — or it might have been for dry cleaning. It gave him a task and a decision. What did it matter whether it was a complex mystery or a simple explanation? He had a free day and the laundry ticket tempted him. He would follow that lead, and if that did not reveal the identity of the dead man he would forget the business and go home.

Printed on the ticket was the name of the laundry and a serial number — no more. There was something important in the little ticket: it had been folded and tucked away. It mattered because it had been forgotten and seemed unintentional. And everything else had appeared so calculated.

He had already stopped thinking of the man as George, and he had been so preoccupied with getting rid of the body that he had not considered what his next move should be.

But this suggestion could hardly have been easier. It was the Wong Hee Laundry on Stuart Street, the China-town exit. If nothing materialized he could just beat it down the turnpike. That was his new guiding thought: See what happens.

It wasn't ghoulish, it was a favor — picking up the dead man's laundry. And Gerald was again reassured by the simplicity of it. It was so easy it could not be wrong.

If he asks, Gerald thought, I'll say I'm Charles Leggate — with an "e" — and my car is double-parked, and I'll have to move it before I can explain how this laundry ticket came into my possession.

And then I'll go underground and never return.

But the elderly Chinese man showed no curiosity and did not even have a polite interest in him. He held the ticket close to his face and matched its number to a large parcel in a tall stack. He handed it over and told Gerald the cost: fourteen dollars. That seemed rather expensive for shirts, which was what he guessed was in the parcel. He went to his car and tore off the wrapper and saw that he was in possession of four linen smocks, folded in tissue paper. They were the sort of white smocks worn by so many people these days, not only dentists, doctors and pharmacists, but also art teachers and certain mechanics who carried out car repairs in the more expensive garages.

If it had been shirts he would have headed straight home. But *smocks?*

He walked back to the laundry and showed the man his ticket.

"I think there was something else in here," he said. "Some shirts."

"No shirts," the man said.

"Can I see the receipt?"

The man nodded and pulled out a shoebox filled with receipts. After a moment of foraging in the box he clawed out the correct piece of paper.

"Four smock," he read. "No starch." He pushed it sourly at Gerald.

Gerald smiled at the success of his ruse. This was what he wanted to see. D. MARR it said in wobbly capital letters, and there was a telephone number.

D. MARR: was that George's alias or just a Chinese mistake in transcription? The smocks he could see had been hand-tailored. They were not standard issue, but rather custom-made. They were as beautiful as surplices — they could have been priestly garments. Could it be that George had become a priest?

Gerald was the only DeMarr in the Boston telephone directory, and no one named Marr was listed. On a hunch — because of the smocks and because the place was so near — Gerald inquired at Tufts Medical School, just across the street. Doctor Marr? Doctor DeMarr? But no such person existed.

He called the telephone number he had memorized from the receipt. It rang repeatedly — hopeless, he thought: he was calling a dead man's number.

"Doctor DeMarr's office." It was a woman's voice, and yet not as crisp as it might have been. Perhaps the answering service?

When it sank in — the Chinese laundry clerk had simply written what he had heard — Gerald said, "Yes, I'd like to speak to the doctor, please."

"I'm afraid that's impossible," the woman said. "He's not available."

"When do you expect him?"

"I'm not sure. Who's speaking, may I ask? Is this Mr. Gubba?"

Without hesitating, Gerald said, "No. I'm a consultant immunologist and I'm just up from Plainfield, New Jersey, for the convention here on immunology and," he took a breath, surprised by his fluency, "I thought I'd look my old friend —"

"So it's not an appointment," the woman said.

"I did want to make an appointment for my wife," Gerald said. "It's rather urgent."

"I was just going to say, we're not taking any new appointments until further notice. Perhaps I can get back to you?"

"It might be easier if I called you back. I'm not sure when I'll be back in Boston. Perhaps I'll write a note. Would you mind giving me your address?"

The woman dictated the address: it was a suite on the fifteenth floor of Riverview Towers, Kenmore Square.

After he hung up, Gerald parked at the Common Garage and went to Kenmore Square in a taxi. Riverview Towers was not a new building, but it was a stately one, of brick and granite, with ornamented stone around its windows and at its edges, and a heavy stone canopy over its front door that somewhat resembled a movie marquee. Gerald counted the floors to fifteen, and he marveled at how he had spent his whole life in that nearby place and had never seen this building or realized that George might still be around. But, thinking about it, he ceased to be surprised; after all, he had always imagined that he had lived a buried life. And now who lay buried?

Still carrying the parcel of smocks — it was like a key to the whole puzzling business — he entered the building and examined the lobby board for names. Among the doctors and dentists, George was listed twice. Gerald gathered that his office was on one floor and his apartment on another. Gerald saw the security guard and thought: I am George's twin — I have a right to be here.

But the security guard did not ask for identification. Gerald smiled to think that George's security could be so lax — and he was probably paying a fortune for this sloppy protection! The guard smiled back at Gerald, and that emboldened him to take the elevator to the fifteenth floor, and he stepped out and saw the brass plate bearing his brother's name. He resisted ringing the bell. Somehow, he knew it was a waiting room, with a five-foot palm tree, and armchairs, and last month's magazines, and a vast meaningless painting on the wall.

He walked up a floor, just to sniff around and see the apartment door, and then he descended to the basement and the parking garage. He prowled on the cool dimly lit floor of cars and saw that the numbered spaces corresponded to the apartment numbers, and that at 1602 there was a Mercedes — lovely, even under its coat of dust. It was a two-seater, light cream with red leather upholstery, and as with the building and the fresh smell of the corridors and the "Doctor," Gerald thought: yes — it all pleased him. And what was oddest was his lack of interest in cars. He drove badly and often said, "I'm car-blind — car-bored, really" — he couldn't tell one from another. But he knew this one, he wanted it, he was happy here and he was gnawed by temptation.

Everything fitted except the man with the puffy and slightly ruined face who had appeared at the house a week ago and said, "Deedee." If he was not in the bag underneath all the soil and seagulls, where was he?

Gerald wanted to go home. It was lunchtime. He could sit and fret quietly. I don't know enough, he thought. That worried him. That meant he knew too much.

In the elevator, he told himself that he had punched the wrong button. He got out at fifteen and told himself that he would get the next elevator down. He sniffed and rang the office bell and told himself that he would not go in, even if someone answered. No one answered. He sniffed again.

That was settled then. He called the elevator and waited, wondering what he would do with this parcel of laundry. He had no use for smocks: he would mail them to this address.

The elevator light went on, the warning bell rang, the doors shot apart and a woman stepped out.

Her stare froze him: she seemed to recognize him, and yet she said nothing. She looked almost fearful, as if she might be wrong. It was an expression he had often seen, though not lately.

This woman had the compact and self-possessed face of a cat, but her skin was sallow and she seemed weary. Gerald saw her eyes flick — she was holding her breath, touching her hair, and in one motion moving her fingertips from her loose blue blouse to her light skirt.

"George." She made it a sharp word, almost a question, and there was a small sob in the way she spoke it.

She had caught him off-guard, and the words he had been rehearsing seemed feeble and unconvincing: Just trying to get some information . . . Looking for my brother . . . Consultant immunologist . . . Found these smocks delivered to my office . . . I called the other day about an appointment . . . Just visiting . . . Has anyone disappeared?

It crossed his mind, just then, that he had killed George and buried him secretly and run off. He was a murderer and his instinct was to conceal what he could and deny everything. The woman's hesitation, her faltering voice, gave him courage and, fingering the parcel and feeling dreadfully guilty, he began to smile.

"Yes," he said. "Are you surprised to see me?"

"No —"

He had made her nervous! But he was annoyed that she didn't know the difference. It was that childhood feeling of discouragement when people ignored him by mistaking him for George.

The woman had turned to the door and was fumbling with the lock, trying to be cheery and apologizing for being late back from lunch.

"Don't worry about it," Gerald said, and stepped inside and thought: He owes me this.

3

He kept on, still sniffing, still sleepwalking, without looking back. He justified himself: I'll get to the bottom of this; then mocked himself with an overtaking thought: It will be over in five minutes.

But he found a reason to feel triumphant. He had not been mistaken for George — no, he had displaced his dead brother. George was almost certainly dead — wasn't this empty office the proof? — and Gerald was no longer a shadow.

The young woman behind him — MISS T. JORDAN was lettered on her desktop nameplate — was speaking in a halting way, trying to begin, "I was getting worried . . ."

"Glad to be back," Gerald said briskly, and didn't turn. She *had* looked worried.

There were other doors at the side of the office — his portion of it. One door led to the examining room, with a high platform-like bed, and a set of scales, and clothes hooks; the room next to it was densely shelved and held bandages and medical supplies — bottles and coils of tubing. Gerald moved swiftly around the office, searching and committing to memory everything he saw — photographs, books, a tray of files, unanswered letters, a diary, an appointment book, and the framed degree displayed on the wall.

He took out a smock and put it on over his shirt and trousers. Now he was more comfortable, more convinced of his right to be there: these were the right clothes.

The wording of the degree was in Latin, but any fool could make out that he was a Doctor of Medicine. So George had graduated from Columbia? There were other certificates on display: he was a member of the American Medical Association, he had been voted Man of the Year — two years ago — and here was a framed badge and scroll testifying that George DeMarr had been an Eagle Scout.

Eagle Scout! Gerald knew this was false. Neither boy had earned the necessary merit badges to achieve that rank. Gerald did not mock, but instead was reminded of a shameful occasion at work when someone had mentioned the Scouts, and he had said, "I was an Eagle Scout . . ."

The phone rang. Gerald wondered whether he ought to answer it. Surely the secretary would pick it up? It continued to ring.

"Yes?"

"It's Tallis."

Tallis?

"You must think I'm crazy," she said. "It's just that you took me by surprise out there . . ."

So Tallis was T. Jordan, the secretary.

Gerald said, "Come in for a moment, will you?"

She was more relaxed this time — she had composed herself — happy to see him safe, he guessed, and also glad that this stranger was in fact the doctor. He knew she felt apologetic for almost not recognizing him, and he was guiltily uneasy, knowing himself to be responsible for her awkwardness.

"I canceled the morning appointments. There were only three. I hadn't heard from you, I had no idea where you were."

"You did the right thing."

"There was another one of those urgent calls this morning."

Another?

"He's going to write you a note," she said. "And that Mr. Gubba was here all morning. He wouldn't go away. Mrs. Florian is scheduled for this afternoon, and so is Mrs. Naishpee — the one with the hyperactive child —"

Tallis broke off, looking troubled, as she had when she had first seen him outside the elevator. She said, "I hope you don't mind my asking this, but is there anything wrong?"

Gerald found it easier to face the woman when he saw that she was disturbed. He could not stand a cold stare or a direct question. If she had been blunt he would have felt very small under his smock. But she was tentative, and so instead of feeling like an imposter he could reassure her. He had merely forgotten part of his past. He did not know what sort of doctor he was, or what his mood should be. He had no driver's license, no keys, no clear image of George the doctor. He knew he seemed vague, but he did not want to stumble so soon. He could not question her. All he knew about this woman was her name. He smiled at her.

He said, "I'm going to tell you something and I want you to swear to me that you will never divulge it to anyone."

"You know you can trust me," she said. "You have plenty of proof."

That meant something.

He said, "And you know you can trust me."

"I think I do now," she said. She smiled, and her smile cost her such effort it seemed to prove the opposite of what she had said — that she had been wounded. "I mean, now that you've come back. I didn't expect it, somehow."

He felt that if he was kind he could rely on her.

"A terrible thing happened to me over the weekend," he said.

Tallis raised her hand involuntarily, as if to protect herself from what he was about to say.

"I had a massive shock," he went on, gaining confidence.

Tallis had become conscious of her raised hand, and now she covered her mouth with it as she listened.

"Don't be frightened," Gerald said — Tallis seemed as if she were about to scream. "I won't tell you what it was. But it's had the most amazing consequences. I feel different, and I have a slight case of amnesia. Certain details, certain objects."

"What have you done to your arm?" she said.

"Nothing," he said, and then remembering how George had died, he added, "Just the usual punishment."

"I see," she said blankly. And then, "Did you say amnesia?"

"Yes, please help me. I don't want anyone to know I've had this unfortunate — this shock. They'll think it's a weakness and try to take advantage of me."

She smiled again, but without effort, without pleasure: it was a memory surfacing in her eyes and mouth. She said, "You haven't changed."

What had he done to make her say that?

"Amnesia would be hilarious if it weren't so inconvenient," Gerald said. "For example, I can't remember what I did with my keys. I couldn't get into my apartment this morning. Maybe I've lost them."

"They arrived last Friday," she said, "with your driver's license and your medical ID. They were found somewhere in Boston and an honest person brought them in. I didn't know where you were, or I would have notified you."

She retrieved a bag of objects from her desk, and the keys inside clanked as she set the bag down on his side table.

She said, "Don't you believe me?"

He wasn't listening.

She said, "There are still some honest people left in the world."

He was thinking: And if I am a doctor, what is my specialty? What do I eat, what do I drink? Am I your lover? But buried in this ignorance was his thrill at not knowing, the risks he was running in being there. That thrill made him incurious and reckless.

He took a step nearer and said, "Tallis."

Her features softened and now he believed what she had told him earlier, about being worried when he hadn't come back. She looked so pale. He meant only to touch her hand, but she took his and clasped it.

"I was feeling desperate," he said.

He had only meant to gain her as an ally, but it seemed to him that she misunderstood. She drew close to him, and then her body rose against his and he could feel her shudder.

Tallis said, "I know what desperation is."

So she had misunderstood; but it was a mistake in his favor. He took it as encouragement, he moved his hand to her arm and helped her closer to him. Beneath her sleeves her arms were so thin! Her pallor and her look of starvation gave her a hungry beauty that Gerald found impossible to separate from illness. He felt mingled pity and desire — he wanted both to feed her and devour her.

She said, "I'm glad you haven't forgotten everything."

"How could I?" he said.

It worked: she gave him a sorrowful grin and said, "I was desperate, too — I felt crazy! Forgive me —"

She suddenly broke free of him and stepped away. She had heard something.

Gerald was about to caress her — of course, he forgave her! — when she said, "It's the two o'clock appointment — Mr. Gubba again, I'm afraid." She was walking toward the outer office.

"Are you still taking appointments?"

"Naturally," she said. She did not turn. "I knew you'd be back."

"I need a little time." He said he was hungry. Would Tallis go out and buy him a sandwich and coffee? He said he'd talk to Mr. Gubba on the office line.

"Listen" — the voice clouted his ear — "you're going to help me this time, ain't you?"

Am I — was George — an abortionist? Gerald wondered. This man's voice sounded both urgent and threatening. "I'll do my best."

"Just do what I want."

He told Mr. Gubba to come back the next day, but he knew that everything depended on his next phone call. The bogus Eagle Scout scroll and medal had been the first clue; and he suspected the Man of the Year award to be merely window dressing. He decided then to verify the most important document.

"Registrar's Office," the voice said.

"I'm inquiring about a certain George DeMarr, who apparently graduated from Columbia Medical School in 1972," Gerald said. He spelled the name and waited until the graduate records were examined. He was transferred to another line; he heard the clack of computer keys and the mutters of another secretary.

"We have no listing under that name."

He tried the Boston branch of the American Medical Association, and was put on hold. He looked at George's driver's license and snorted at the mug shot. How could Tallis have been taken in? There was no resemblance at all! But he felt there was justice in this, and it was the fact that he was certain to be exposed as an imposter that made him bold. He would fail, of course — he would wake up from this — and it would be a glorious failure, a wonderful awakening.

But in the meantime he deserved a period of successful stealth. He had spent his whole life meagerly as the dim half of a double image, and it was only today that he had felt any excitement in living. It was like coming back from a sort of underground prison. He did not care about living George's life. I want to live my own, he thought — the one I've been denied.

"I'm sorry to keep you. We have no one of that name in this AMA branch. Perhaps it's a new entry —"

This was excellent news, and it excited a responsive feeling in Gerald: with each succeeding falsehood connected with George, the more confidence he had in his own truth. Tallis, in those moments beside him, had helped, too. By returning his affection she had made him believe in himself: he hadn't faked the affection — he really had wanted to put his mouth on her.

And he liked the risk — liked it best because it did not matter whether he failed. Even if it all ended now with this patient saying "What have you done with Doctor DeMarr!" it would be worth it, because he had discovered something that delighted him. George was no doctor — his degree was a forgery. George himself was an imposter!

Gerald ate his sandwich by the window, and then drank his coffee, and carefully brushed his teeth. George was a quack! He dialed Tallis and said, "Send in the next patient, please."

She was Mrs. Florian, a square-faced woman with beautiful eyes. In her dark dress she seemed heavy, and she moved slowly, staying stiffly upright and using her shoulders in a way that attempted sensuality without quite achieving the effect. It was only when she was seated that her sadness was evident, and then she looked lumpish and stubborn. She brought a strong aroma of syrupy perfume into the room, and there was a pattern on her dress, glittering on the dark silk, of dead birds.

Her file lay before him — the typed particulars and nearly illegible notes.

Mrs. Florian said, "I thought your watch dog wasn't going to let me see you," and she moved her eyes meaningfully without moving her body.

Gerald smiled in the direction of the outer office, where Tallis sat beneath the seven-foot tree — he had been right about that and the bad painting, too!

"She said you were busy. That always means something, because busy doesn't mean anything."

Gerald said, "I've had a heavy week."

"I thought she meant you were sick. And then I started wondering who your doctor is. I thought, 'Why should I go to him? I should go to *his* doctor!' "

Gerald said, "I look after myself."

But Mrs. Florian seemed bored as soon as he began to speak. She folded her arms and Gerald guessed that she was referring to her ailment when she said, "I did what you told me."

"You did? That's excellent." He set his face at her benignly in an effort to hide the fact that he was totally mystified.

"And it didn't work."

"What a shame."

"So you were wrong."

She was playing a role — using pauses and coyness. That made it especially difficult for him, because he was concentrating hard, hoping for a clue.

Her eyes were deep-set and though they were large they had an oriental cast to them — it was their loveliness — they gave nothing away. Gerald could see pleasure in the pout of her jowls: she was enjoying this.

"And you were so sure of yourself!" she said.

It was a self-satisfied tone — not quite triumphant — and the gloating in it was friendly rather than belittling. It was a sort of bullying intimacy, and it confused Gerald. He wished he had been able to decipher the scribbles in her file.

Mrs. Florian said, "I think it might have made my condition worse."

Made what condition worse?

"That's extremely," he began in a ponderous way, and paused, inviting the woman to interrupt.

"I understand how cutting down on smoking might help," she said, filling the silence he had created for her. "As you suggested."

This was a start. Gerald said, "It was only a suggestion."

"But don't you see how the anxiety of going without cigarettes might have irritated it more?"

Irritated what more?

Gerald shrugged, and she said, "Isn't there anything I can take for it?"

"There are many things you could take, but will they do you any good? I'm not sure what the best answer is."

Because I don't know the question.

Mrs. Florian said, "I've been getting these sharp pains again in the upper abdominal region, and I know it's not peritonitis — we've been through that, haven't we? Sometimes it's agony. Can't you x-ray it?"

"It doesn't always show up on an x-ray."

"Even with barium?"

He was very grateful to her for this. He said, "Barium's a funny thing. It doesn't always behave itself."

"Drink lots of milk. That's what my mother would say," Mrs. Florian said. "But what did she know about ulcers?"

Ah. Gerald said, "Some of these folk remedies can be very effective. Milk's not a bad idea. With ulcers you have to be very careful in your diet. And alcohol — particularly on an empty stomach —"

Hearing this, Mrs. Florian began to look hurt and slightly guilty. She said, "I'm obsessive about what I put into my body. I don't eat junk. I don't drink crap. If you want to know, I'm kind of a fanatic."

She was a big solid woman who, seated, seemed like part of the chair. She was apparently alone and unhappy, and she had the powerful appetite that compensated for a friend in some solitary people. Her loneliness had made her a stuffer. And she was so wounded by Gerald's remark about drinking that he was almost sure she was lying.

He said, "Obviously, you take care of yourself. That's very important."

"Worrying about ulcers can give you ulcers!"

"Now this is very true," Gerald said. He did not know how to go on from this. He smiled at her. She was calmer now. He said, "Was there anything else?"

She looked amused and resentful, as if he were trying to hurry her.

"Aren't you going to examine me?"

"Ulcers are very hard to examine."

"There's a sort of swelling," she said.

"Let's have a look," Gerald said.

She rose and went to the examining room: she had done this many times; she knew the moves. Gerald heard her sigh as she removed her clothes, and there was something coquettish in the way she sweetened her voice and said, "Ready."

She was naked under a short paper smock that she had found somewhere in the room, and she lay on the examining table like a badly wrapped parcel — a body in a small paper sack. Her arms were behind her head and her knees drawn up. Where she was not blackly tanned she was puffy and mutton-colored, and this unnerved Gerald more than the dead flesh of the corpse he had found in his house and tipped into the dump at Cape Cod.

He fumbled with his stethoscope — listened; fumbled with his watch — felt her wrist; then he grunted and touched Mrs. Florian under her breasts, his fingers spread as if playing a chord on her ribs.

"A bit lower."

He moved his fingertips as she suggested.

"Do you feel anything?"

She said, "Don't *you?*"

He said gently, "I see what you mean," and stepped back, so that she could see him in a reflective mood, pondering her symptoms.

"You can put your clothes on," he said.

"Aren't you going to palpate me?"

"Of course," he said, and approached her frowning in order to look serious: he did not want to betray his bafflement. *Palpate?*

She opened her legs and they made a smacking sound as if she was unsticking her thighs. Her face was turned aside: he hoped she wasn't smiling. He touched her tentatively, then tried again. He knew now that she could not pretend — he was nervous, and she knew.

"What's the hurry, Doctor?"

He wanted to say: *Don't you see? I'm not the Doctor!*

She said, "You're always in a hurry."

Always!

He said, "I'm sorry."

"You always say that."

And then he knew he had succeeded.

The next patient was a woman with a damaged face, Muriel Dietrich. He hoped that she had not come to him about her face. She had not. She wanted him to sign an application that would allow her a license plate saying that she was handicapped. She said that she could never find a parking place and was sick of walking two miles every time she came into Boston.

"They ask me to describe your handicap," Gerald said, examining the form.

"Old age — that's the worst handicap of all, God help me," she said. "You know what to write."

He invented a disease and created a Latin name for it,

and he defined it in parentheses: "Progressive wasting."
He was pleased to be able to conspire with this woman
against the young traffic cops.

Mr. Lombardi — another — said he had emphysema. It
was an illness Gerald had heard about. He wondered
whether Mr. Lombardi was telling the truth when he
described how he could not breathe and how he slept
badly. He coughed terribly, he said. He used the word
"sputum." "I throw up every morning," he said. He
reeked of cigar smoke.

His file showed that George had been treating him for
three years for various ailments.

"I'm still taking the medication," Mr. Lombardi said.

He too demanded to be examined.

Gerald took his time and afterward said, "Come back
and see me after another three thousand miles." This delighted Mr. Lombardi.

"It's my skin tabs," Mrs. Brewster said.

She had come with her husband, an overweight and
bosomy man, sixty or so, who had his wife's way of
clasping his hands between his knees. He said nothing.
When his wife spoke he became nervous and his eyes
twitched in flutter-fits of blinking.

Mrs. Brewster was asking to be treated with the latest
methods. She demanded laser beams.

As she was being examined, she said, "There's something different about you."

This made Gerald wary.

"You look happy," she said.

Ms. Frezza made the same comment. She was thirty, she
was "spotting." It was the Pill, she said.

They were experts on what ailed them. They described their symptoms, they guessed at causes, they suggested remedies. Their physical condition did not match their complaints: they all seemed fairly healthy. Gerald decided that they were reporting progress — they felt a little worse, a little better. Gerald listened carefully and tried to be sympathetic. The rest was ritual — the stethoscope, the tapped lungs, the deep breathing, the pulse-taking, the simple rubber bulb device for checking blood pressure.

Gerald saw that they were not looking for advice. They were suspiciously full of information. They were looking for agreement. Most of all they were in the mood for more medication, and three of them demanded prescriptions.

Between Lombardi and Brewster there had been a phone call.

"You were recommended," the voice said. It was a tentative request, but when Gerald encouraged him he stated it. "Thought you might be able to write me a prescription. I'll pay the going rate — I know you're not cheap. The thing is, I've got to have it right away —"

They were not really sick, Gerald thought — and as for Mrs. Naishpee and her ten-year-old son, diagnosed as hyperactive: She was a heavy woman with a drugged and drawling voice that Gerald found maddening. Her child was practically a monkey, but it was not hard to explain how he had gotten that way. Mrs. Naishpee, too, wanted more medication.

Prescriptions were the one item he could not provide

— later, perhaps, as he told the man on the phone (who angrily swore at him and hung up). He could not write them, he had no knowledge of drugs, he could not even find George's prescription pad.

But that was his only problem, and it was a small one. He had begun in the confidence that George had been a phony. Seeing patients was slow work — they were so talkative! But Gerald's natural nervousness had kept him going and made him attentive. He watched the patients closely, alert to everything they said. They were very calm. They were uninterested in him. They had the selfish concentration of people who believe themselves to be unwell. They were ordinary people whose imagined illnesses had made them superstitious and turned them into egotists. By the end of the day's appointments Gerald was sure that everyone he had seen was a hypochondriac. It seemed hugely appropriate that each one had come here to see Doctor DeMarr, for who was better at treating a hypochondriac than a quack?

When there were no more patients, Gerald could think clearly — and it was then that he realized that he had not consciously tried to imitate George. He had not been aware of impersonating his brother. He had been himself, without any pretense. It was his own triumph — George had had no part in it. Gerald's skill was his common sense. It was not necessary to think about George. But when he reflected on his success he decided that it had not arisen out of imitation but was instead a result of his having improved upon

George. He was, simply, better than his brother: "There's something different . . . You're happy."

The day had started with a burial; but that burial had set him free.

He could not show his delight. He didn't dare. And yet his feeling of satisfaction relaxed him and made him solemnly garrulous — he wanted to take that woman Tallis into his confidence.

"I think I should tell you the reason for my shock," he said. She had come into his office with the same suffering look that had touched his heart when he had first seen her. He realized that she was the first young person he had ever wanted to help.

She said, "It's not necessary —"

"Please, stay."

She turned to him, looking apprehensive. "If it'll make you feel better."

"It was my brother. He died over the weekend."

He was then very sorry he had said it. Tallis looked stunned, and Gerald imagined for a moment that she had stopped breathing. He saw how thin she was — so frail in her summer clothes — and he saw, too, a stiffness, a teetering resignation. Tallis looked like someone who had just drowned.

"Are you all right?" he said. He found himself reassuring her.

She said in a slow, underwater voice, "I didn't even know you had a brother."

4

He had taken possession of the office; now he unlocked the door of George's apartment and sized it up. It was empty and cool on this summer evening, and its stillness said that it had been abandoned. It was hard to be in a dead man's home and not think that you were in a tomb: it brought back his sad old buried-alive feeling.

The place was very orderly, and moving from room to room Gerald saw that George had lived here alone. It was obvious in the undisturbed order of the rooms, the walled-in shadows, the position of the one large chair, the single taste in the décor — orangey walls, an unlikely terracotta color that was, Gerald thought, perfect really. The bathroom — everything in it — told him that only one person used it, a vain and rather foolish man who pampered himself in a superficial and self-deceiving way and lingered here in that silk bathrobe, among these mirrors and these expensive bottles, looking at his own awful face.

George was dead. Gerald searched the rooms for drugs. Perhaps there were none here; perhaps they were well hidden. In any case, it was a mistake he had no intention of making — it had killed George, so it would save him: George's death gave me life.

Apart from the drugs, George's life had been fairly tidy. Gerald saw that he could make it perfect.

He found the liquor cabinet and poured himself a glass of vodka. He threw the windows open for the evening breeze. He was high enough so that the street noise was muffled, even somewhat comforting — a low clatter and drone, adding to the raffish atmosphere of this downtown apartment. The bedroom had a textile smell — curtains and bedspread, and what were those ridiculous candles doing on the dresser? But when Gerald lit them he saw the room in a new way, the flames jumping on the wall, the mirrors on the headboard of the bed glittering, and he savored the tang of warm wax. He filled his glass again and tried to resist gulping it. But his thirst was powerful — all those years of dullness and denial, his shadow life as a twin. He drank and soon he possessed the apartment. I deserve this.

Before he was fully drunk he took a shower, believing it would sober him. He changed into one of George's lightweight suits. What pleasure it gave him to pull on those socks and slip on the jacket — a perfect fit. The low chair was just the right height.

He thought: It had to be George, because he was small enough to fit into the barrel.

He instantly forgot that thought.

What am I trying to remember?

Something — a crystal — began to form from broken splinters in his mind. He took another drink to help it along, and then he sensed it dissolve. He was glad it was gone. He suspected that it had been a fear.

The phone rang. He was laughing softly as he answered it.

It was Tallis. Already this life seemed wholly circumscribed!

"I hope you don't think I was being insensitive. I am very sorry about your brother. If I had known he existed I think I might have been able to say something sensible. But it was such a surprise — that you had a brother, that he was dead."

Gerald said, "Why not come over?"

His triumphant feeling, which was a feeling of wonderful lungs, had returned to him with her call.

"Would it help?" She was thinking of the death. In a guarded way she said, "I'm still a little afraid of you. And it's late."

He was glad she said that, because he was a little afraid of her. But she had spoken first: he felt protected by her fear.

He said, "The way you touched me today —"

There was a sound of air in the phone — had she sighed?

He said, "I felt like someone completely different. I was alive, in a kind of time warp. Nothing else mattered. I wanted you so much. You'll never know how that re-assured me. Energy passed through your hand and strengthened me, and —"

He faltered, becoming self-conscious at her prolonged silence and wondering how long he had been talking — was it minutes or hours? He felt enlarged and noisy and stupid with vodka. He was afraid in a helpless way that he had gone too far with her and had been talking through his hat.

Still she said nothing.

"Are you there?"

He forgot her name.

"Yes," she said. "It's strange hearing you say that."

Had he blundered?

"That was one of the first things you ever said to me."

What had he said?

"You're so sweet, George," she said sorrowfully.

This was perfection. What was it the woman patient had said? *You always say that.* Perfection.

Tallis said, "You have changed, haven't you?"

"Yes, yes," he said. "What is it?"

She was crying now, but in trying to stifle the sobs she was making them more distinct.

"You know what I need," she said at last.

But her sobs had frightened him. He said, "Maybe you're right. It is pretty late."

"You've got a terrible day tomorrow," she said.

Another mystery. He said, "Excuse me?" pretending he hadn't heard it, so that she would rephrase it — perhaps explain it.

"Those scary-looking guys are coming tomorrow," she said.

That didn't help.

"But I'm pretty desperate, too. What about tomorrow night? If you really mean it."

"I mean it!"

In saying so he convinced himself that he had known her for years and understood her. And as if to prove it, in that same moment he remembered her name.

"I mean it, Tallis."

"We'll do it the old way and take our time, like we used to."

"Yes," he said, "like we used to," and saw it all — candles, mirrors, her long pale body in his bed, and her shadow making a witch on the wall — a witch riding a broomstick.

He was asleep soon after that, and all night the roaring in his ears from the traffic in Kenmore Square had a sound like a slipstream and gave him dreams.

J ust before he woke he dreamed of a woman whom he was passing on Boylston Street. "What are you doing here?" she mouthed. She was small and old, she had a child's face. She drew a gun from out of her oversize coat and shot Gerald in the chest. He ran slowly, sinking to his knees with each step. It was a toy pistol — he had known that before it went off — and yet the woman's face had terrified him. The woman was his mother.

While he was dressing the dream came to him — the pistol first, then the rest of it. But what fascinated him was the realization that he had had that same dream ten thousand times or more. He just now grasped that he had been dreaming it most nights of his life.

A patient was waiting in the reception area. This was the reason Tallis greeted Gerald in a formal way.

"Good morning, Doctor."

Gerald smiled, thinking: Doctor of what?

But he was pleased. There was something about Tallis's formality that suggested there was passion beneath it — exactly like the fine gray suit she had on: it was for him. She was being efficient, giving nothing away; it distracted and aroused him.

She has made love to me before, he thought. Soon, I'll make love to her.

"Any messages?" he said. When she handed over the sheaf of pink slips he muttered, "Prescriptions, prescriptions."

She said, "Are you surprised?"

"I couldn't find my prescription pad yesterday," he said.

"On your desk."

"No" — he had looked for it, he was absolutely sure.

Today the pad lay at the corner of the blotter. Gerald thought: I must be careful.

The patient was Murray U. Stone. Gerald saw from his file that he was eighty-six years old. He was full of complaints — back pains, indigestion, sleeplessness, wind. How strange that this man on the verge of death should care about his stomach and his sleep — he was snatching at another month of life. The old man thought it might be his prostate — that was the sort of thing he had to expect at his time of life, wasn't it?

Gerald quizzed him on his diet and told him to cut down on ice cream.

Mr. Stone wanted to go on living. Two days earlier, Gerald would have found this pointless and selfish, and in an old man a kind of insanity. Now he saw the point of it. He sympathized with the trembling man. It wasn't such a crazy wish, and Gerald was all the more attentive when he remembered the humiliation and boredom of his other life.

"Aren't you going to have a poke at my prostate?" the old man said.

In time, Gerald thought, I will understand this business. But it was not a job — it was a whole life. Already he had begun to accept its demands. He was glad of that: he wanted to live this life. But there were certain tasks he could not perform. He could not carry out a convincing examination, he was too disgusted by the sight of their underwear to be able to concentrate; he couldn't write prescriptions, he knew nothing of drugs.

He was often made speechless, or at least short of breath, by their nakedness. Poor pale flesh — it did not fit them. So he stalled. He played charades with the stethoscope, he muttered. He sent Mr. Stone away with a tube of ointment he had found in a box of samples.

Mr. Libby, the next patient, entered the office bent double, as if he was straining to touch his toes. He stayed in this stooped position, speaking sideways about wanting to see a chiropractor.

Gerald was genuinely annoyed that Mr. Libby wanted to be recommended to a specialist. He said, "Don't you trust me to treat you?" and fished out a bottle of Valium from among the samples.

"Valium's for depression," Mr. Libby said.

"It has many uses," Gerald said in a peevish way. It was the one drug he understood and this stupid man was contradicting him! "It relaxes muscles — all muscles. That's why it's good for tension, that's why it's good for bad backs. Don't you want to get better?"

There were phone calls after that — demands for prescriptions. They made him feel inadequate. He considered taking a vacation — maybe to Florida, where he could bribe a pharmacist to show him how to write prescriptions for the important drugs. With a professional letterhead on his pad and a medical degree on the wall, he could make it all look legitimate. And he was prepared to pay thousands — it was an investment. A pharmacist would probably be very glad of the chance to make that kind of money. It was not dishonest, he felt — it was just complicated and hard to explain. But it was idealism all the same. He saw it clearly, and then it struck him that it was exactly what George had done.

I'll find another way, he thought.

That was the morning. He was wondering whether to go out for lunch when Tallis buzzed him and said in a whisper, "Mr. Gubba's just gotten out of the elevator."

He heard the thump of the reception room door and, almost in the same moment, his own door was shoved open and the man was upon him, with Tallis close behind, handing Gerald the man's file.

Mr. Gubba was young and haggard. He had a gray complexion and yellowish eyes, and he limped — but he seemed careless rather than crippled. He was thin and round-shouldered, like an awkward boy. His hair was tangled, he needed a shave. He wore a wrinkled shirt, and it was from the pocket of this that he took a folded-over swatch of twenty-dollar bills. He placed the money on the desk.

"I'm not going to argue with you this time," Mr. Gubba said. "Just give me the prescription and I'll go."

"You'll have to be a bit more specific," Gerald said.

"You know what I'm talking about."

The gaps between his teeth seemed to indicate that he was unintelligent. Yet the man was persistent and oddly energetic — dry-mouthed in a nervous sort of way, but defiant, like all the other hypochondriacs he had seen in this office. But which others had tried to palm money to him?

"I've been having a hard time," Mr. Gubba said.

Gerald had concealed the file, but even so there was nothing on it when he quietly sneaked a look — the name and address, nothing else; no record of illnesses, no prescriptions.

Mr. Gubba was still talking: "And these doctors you recommended — they wouldn't give me anything."

"I'm sorry about that," Gerald said, trying to calm the man with a show of sympathy.

"And you went away," Mr. Gubba said. "I was sick. I didn't know what to do."

"Let's have a look at you," Gerald said, and reached for his stethoscope.

This made Mr. Gubba angry. "You're always doing that. You're stalling. You're wasting my time. Are you going to give me a prescription or not?"

Gerald said in a kindly way, "I can't give you anything at the moment."

"I told you the last time, I'm running out of stuff. I won't have any in a few days — and then what?" But he did not wait for a reply. He said, "It's not fair!"

Gerald said, "I want to help —"

"You *have* to help," Mr. Gubba said. "You gave prescriptions to three people I know, four hundred bucks apiece. This is five hundred, Doctor —"

"I don't want your money."

"Rizzo — you gave him one. I seen it!" Mr. Gubba stood up, and even though Gerald himself was standing the man towered over him. "I could pinch your head off so easy."

For the first time, Gerald became frightened. The man was doing much more than demanding a prescription — he was threatening harm. Mr. Gubba was a desperate, sick-looking man with crazy eyes, and he obviously wanted a drug, some narcotic or other. Gerald wanted to help him, but how? He could not write a prescription, he did not know anything about narcotics. He could humor a patient, but this was something different: he was helpless.

"And a guy named Ferrara. You gave him one!"

Who were these people and what had he given them?

Gerald moved away from Mr. Gubba, to place a safe distance between them. He did not want to argue. He wanted the money, he wanted this life, and he already hated this man enough to give him exactly what he wanted, and the more lethal the better. But he resisted. This was precisely where George had gone wrong.

"You'll have to go," Gerald said.

"I'm not moving."

"I'll call the police."

"Beautiful," Mr. Gubba said. "Then I'll tell the police about all the shit you got for these other guys."

"If you do," Gerald said crisply, inspired by his anger, "I'll never get anything for you. Are you willing to risk that?"

Mr. Gubba stood up. He said, "I'll be back."

It was a snarl, a threat — he spoke it darkly; and it rattled Gerald terribly. It was now after two o'clock, with another patient on the way. There was no time for lunch.

The next patient had a similar request to Mr. Gubba's. This was Toby — another blank file: he was underweight, twenty or so, with a skeletal smile: clearly ill and addicted. He said, "How about it?"

"I can't help you," Gerald said.

"That's what you said the last time."

Good, Gerald thought. He said, "I want you to understand that."

"I don't understand nothing. You cost me a lot of

money. I paid for this office. That desk. That crappy lamp. That's my money."

Gerald resented the young man's tone, and the mention of the lamp — he particularly liked that stainless steel desk lamp. There was much in the office that he realized he had wanted his whole life.

"I can't give you a prescription," he said.

"I think you like saying that. It gives you a sense of power. You're paranoid."

Gerald hated ignorant people who used pompous words to intimidate him. The young man was stupid, and yet Gerald was still hurt by his insolence. He suspected that it did not arise from the young man's own weakness but rather from his seeing that Gerald was helpless.

"Your time is up," Gerald said, feeling trapped.

"I'm leaving, but I'm not going anywhere. Get it?" He stood up. "I'll be around."

There was another phone call: "You were recommended." There was a man named Hume who said the pimple on the back of his neck was a boil that needed lancing. And there was Archdale.

Archdale was a Harvard student; he looked pathetic with his thick grubby textbooks, and Gerald knew before the boy spoke that he wanted a prescription. Archdale pleaded. He had money with him, he said. He looked worried and began to cry, saying that he might be able to get more.

"Please," Gerald said. He wondered whether he should offer to examine him. He was afraid to touch him.

He said, "You've been here before, haven't you?"

"Yes —"

And then Gerald saw that it was in this that George had gone wrong. He thought: I will not become George.

Archdale said, "I was going to kill myself last night."

"That's not an answer," Gerald said.

Archdale had not heard him. He was still talking, saying, "I realized what it was. You didn't want money anymore. You say no —"

Had George said no?

"It's very smart, really. It's a kind of strength, saying you don't want money anymore."

Gerald did not know what to say.

"I can't buy you, because you've already got money," Archdale said. "But ask yourself — how did you make all that money?"

Now the young man was going, but he paused at the door.

"Ask yourself."

When the young man was gone, Gerald was so shaken he told Tallis that he could not see any more patients. He had begun to understand how messy George's life had been: he did not want to make the same mistakes. He needed time, in order to succeed.

He said, "I'm going up to my apartment."

"What time do you want to meet?"

He had forgotten that — anxiety had taken away his desire. He wanted to be alone, but he did not have the heart to tell her. What would George have done?

He said, as candidly as he could, "I'm not sure about tonight."

"What do you mean by that?"

He was vague because he was tired and fearful, but she seemed to think it was a lack of interest.

Before he could reply, Tallis said coldly, "I never know whether to trust you."

"You can trust me," he said, trying hard to reassure her.

She smiled. She said, "You let me down once." Her smile broke and she began to cry. The weeping had a ruinous effect on her. She looked then like one of the most unhealthy people he had ever seen, and a great deal sicker than any of his patients.

He felt pity for her. No other person so young had ever moved him in that way. She was shattered, and George had borne some responsibility for her condition. But Gerald would heal her: it was the crucial difference between his brother and himself.

"I will help you," he said. "But I may not be able to see you tonight."

She was asking him why with her tragic face. He did not want to tell her he was afraid. He said nothing.

Tallis said with a sudden bitterness, "I thought you'd changed."

"I *have* changed," he said, trusting the truth of it: He was a different man! "I'll prove it. Tomorrow —"

"I don't think I can wait until tomorrow," Tallis said. She watched him hurry to the door. She said, "You're going again."

"It's very important!"

She didn't blink. She said, "That's what you said the last time."

5

It was in East Boston — according to the file — a sharp right turn after the tunnel, all tenements and hanging laundry, and big badly made houses intersected by narrow streets. He had left the taxi at the first set of traffic lights, and now he was walking. From the airport came the roar and boom of planes, but here the nighttime noises were clear voices, dishes being clanked in a sink, television laughter in little bursts of pressure, and the whispers of people in the darkness of their porches and front steps. The sounds were un-self-conscious and strangely intimate. The neighborhood was poor Italian; it smelled of laundry and cooking — scorched tomatoes especially. The dark cluttered air gave Gerald the sense that he was walking under water.

He turned the corner and saw the house. The newness

of it surprised him: it was in bright repair. In a row of tall square-sided tenements, wood-framed, with dingy scratched shingles on their fronts, this house had white-trimmed windows and fringed awnings, a screened-in piazza and brick steps. It was a proud little bungalow. Gerald was bewildered and somewhat encouraged by it.

He had been frightened. He had gone there wondering what decision to take. If the house had been a decaying brown tenement he might have been too fearful to knock, he would have gone away. But his curiosity overcame his timidity: the house did not tally with the man. He had not decided what to say, but now at least he could discuss matters. He wanted to help; he did not want to make George's mistakes. The threat had truly terrified him.

Walking past it, he saw movement inside — people behind curtains, a woman in a kitchen window, and in another room a flickering blue fluorescence on the ceiling reflecting a television screen.

He could make a deal — just a simple deal. He would not procure the drugs, but instead would offer to sell him some prescription blanks — or give them to him, providing he used them in another city, providing he would say he had stolen them if he were arrested, providing there were no more threats. It was a compromise, but it made sense and Gerald felt it might rid him of the man.

Gerald was relieved that he could not push drugs onto the young man, because he disliked him enough to do it; he was tempted. Yet he did not have to worry about the morality of it, or the fact that it was crooked. He did not have the skill to write prescriptions.

He rang the bell. He heard, "I'll get it!"

A small boy came to the door. His T-shirt said RED SOX.

"I want to speak to Mr. Gubba," Gerald said through the mesh in the screen door.

"Daddy!" the boy yelled, turning his back on Gerald.

Standing on the front steps in the darkness, Gerald could see into the house, past the entryway to the foyer and a long corridor. The man did not appear. The child ran to the far end of the corridor, and yelled again.

There he was. Gerald watched with fascination as the man walked down the corridor. Something very private and self-contained was apparent in his posture. He was not the starved wolf of the afternoon, but a relaxed husband and father who had been interrupted while reading his newspaper — it was in his hand; he carried it suspended lightly like a piece of cloth. He was clean-shaven, his hair was combed — he had the rosy just-peeled look of someone who was still damp and pink from his shower. He wore a sport shirt and yellow slacks, and even barefoot he looked dapper. It was Mr. Gubba — transformed.

Seeing him, Gerald stepped back — down the stairs and onto the sidewalk. He decided to run, but just a fraction too late: Mr. Gubba got a glimpse of his face a moment before Gerald dashed down the street.

"What are you doing here!"

Gerald ran, in a panicky way, frightened by the slap of his feet on the sidewalk. Later, after he was safe in a taxi and speeding through the tunnel, he remembered that the barefoot man could never have caught him. He had another recollection — that it had all happened before: he had experienced that whole episode — discovery and chase — from an old dream.

He went to Kenmore Square, but only to get rid of his brother's unlucky clothes and to find a telephone number.

"It's me," he said. He did not want to say George. That was over.

Tallis said, "What's wrong? Where have you been? Why do you sound so —"

"I've just found Gubba," he said. Tallis said nothing. He said, "Did you hear me?"

"I heard you." Her voice had gone cold.

"Tallis — he's a phony. He's completely different. He's either a cop or an informer!"

He was struggling against her silence.

"Are you listening?"

Tallis said, "Where have you really been?"

"I'm trying to tell you. Gubba's house. I saw him at home!"

"You've got to be lying."

"He was trying to set me up!" Gerald said. "He's no junkie. He wanted to get me arrested."

She said, "Do we have to go through all of this again?"

"It's serious."

"Yes, but it's not news. You knew what Gubba was up to. You're making excuses."

"I'm scared, Tallis."

She said, "Exactly what you said before, when you ran out on me."

He could not speak.

She said, "You haven't changed at all. You really have lost your nerve."

"I have changed," he said. "I'm going straight — no more phony prescriptions, no more lies. I'm going to live right. And I'll tell you something else: I've stopped taking drugs."

She said, "When did you *start?*"

Before he could react she spoke again. "I've got to see you. Please don't go away again. You said we could meet — we're lucky to have another chance, George —"

George is dead, he thought. I am alive. Being George had given him a taste for life. Before, the thought of dying had not worried him. But now he wanted to live; so he bolted.

He found his old car in the Common Garage. The sense of desperation was still vivid in his mind. George must have felt this way — no, George had felt worse: George was George, and Gerald was himself. George had been fleeing his only life. Gerald felt some sympathy for his brother now, and when he reached home and locked the door and washed he looked into the mirror over the sink and saw a resemblance. It must have been something like the face that George had seen in his own mirror. In Gerald's pity there was smugness and relief: he was home, he was safe. He thought: I'm not dead.

And yet he did not sleep well. He had slept much more soundly last night in George's bed. He thrashed, trying to dive and submerge himself in sleep, but each time he ended up bobbing on his back, awake, his face to the ceiling, watching the car headlights move from one side to the other.

An hour passed; another hour. One set of headlights moved more slowly than the others, then stopped before they reached the far wall. They slid on the ceiling until they were over Gerald's bed. He sat up and listened.

The car had entered his driveway. Gerald looked out and saw only shadows inside, though just after turning away from the window he thought he heard the click of a car door being shut very carefully.

Gerald did not bother to dress. He hurried to the back stairs and climbed to the empty apartment on the upper floor where George had been. There he waited, wondering whether to sit down in that dreadful chair. Let them take what they want, he thought, and then he sat down.

He covered his face: My poor brother. He was thinking about himself most of all. He was both of them. And he always felt especially small in the early morning.

Dawn had reached the windows — a yellow-green early morning sky behind the telephone poles, that forest of black crucifixes. There was no sun yet, but instead pale seeping colors that brimmed like liquid around the old house.

The door opened quickly and a large startled man said, "You're still here."

Then Gerald was dazzled by the man's flashlight, and the weak sunrise was not strong enough to outshine it. The man was hidden behind it and, perhaps realizing what he had just said, he repeated it in amazement: "You're still here!"

The light shook as it moved toward Gerald, paralyzing and blinding him. He was at the mercy of the man, but the man was breathless — still exclaiming, and almost laughing as he spoke.

"I'm alive," Gerald said.

"Course you are."

"Turn off the light — please."

The man did so. Gerald saw that this large dark man had a short neck — no neck at all really; his head was crammed between his shoulders, and when he turned his head he turned his whole body. But he had the sleepy friendly look of someone who has just woken up. He was still on the verge of laughter, with eager eyes, as if he was listening to a good story and wanting more.

"You know me," he said. "Right?"

"No," Gerald said, and felt safe.

"You don't know me!"

Now the man did laugh, and watching him, Gerald laughed, too. It was a good joke — after all he had been through, he was relieved by the apparition of the laughing man.

Gerald pondered the situation: I think I know this man. I think I have been here before.

The intimation had been frequent over the past two days: his dreams had prepared him and had made this strangeness familiar. He was sure he had dreamed this: the empty room, the visiting man, the pale sky, the stillness — and even the man's unexpected laughter. He had seen it all, more than once.

"Why ain't you asleep?"

That sounded familiar, too!

And when Gerald said, "I couldn't sleep," it sounded to him like another echo.

The man's face was bright — he was smiling, perhaps thinking: He should be in bed! There were footsteps on the back stairs. The man wasn't alarmed. He walked easily over to the door and opened it to the visitor.

"Tallis," Gerald said.

Her face was sallow and bony, her clothes were shapeless on her body — they hung in vertical folds. Her thin ankles showed at her trouser cuffs and her little toes were twisted in her sandals.

"He's still here. He says he doesn't know me," the man said.

Tallis smiled at this — the smile tightened her face and made it even thinner. She approached Gerald with her hands in her pockets.

Gerald said, "You're going to laugh when I tell you — you're laughing already."

Only seconds had passed since she had entered the room. But Gerald was fascinated by her. She was all he wanted of George's life. She was lovely in a pitiful way and she looked hungrily at him — still smiling slightly. She had lovely lips and large eyes: they were part of her hunger.

Tallis drew her hand out of her pocket and Gerald saw something between her fingers. She lifted her hand and her sleeve slipped back; he saw scars and blue punctures where her sleeve had been. She held the pointed thing like a dart. It was so narrow and she was so nimble with it, it seemed like part of her hand. She found the plunger with her thumb and let the needle glitter at him.

"Now I'll show you how it's done," Tallis said. "But this time you don't wake up."

"Are you talking to me?" Gerald said.

"Both of you," she said.

He thought for a moment that she meant George and him — the idea of George still clung to him, and he had been dragging his brother around like a flat shadow. But no — she meant the man, who was now behind him. Gerald turned and saw that the man, still smiling, had raised his hands and spread his thick fingers to take hold of him.

Gerald said, "Wait."

He desperately needed time to finish a new thought. It was a recent memory. In George's shoes he saw that George had been right. They only had one life, and it meant one thing — the same life, the same death.